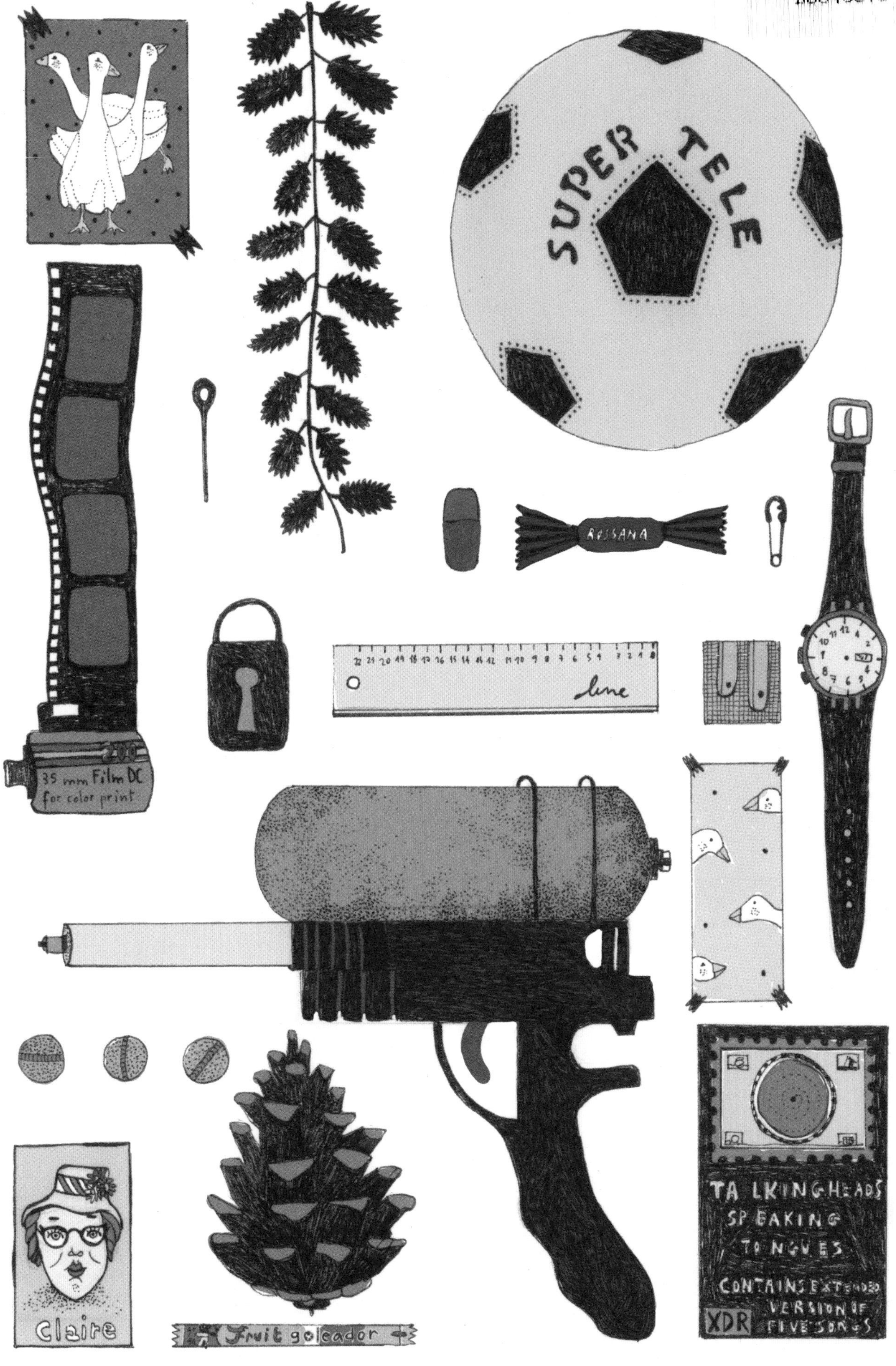

SUPER TELE
ROSSANA
line
200
35 mm Film DC
for color print
Claire
Fruit goleador
TALKINGHEADS
SPEAKING
TONGUES
CONTAINS EXTENDED
VERSION OF
FIVE SONGS
XDR

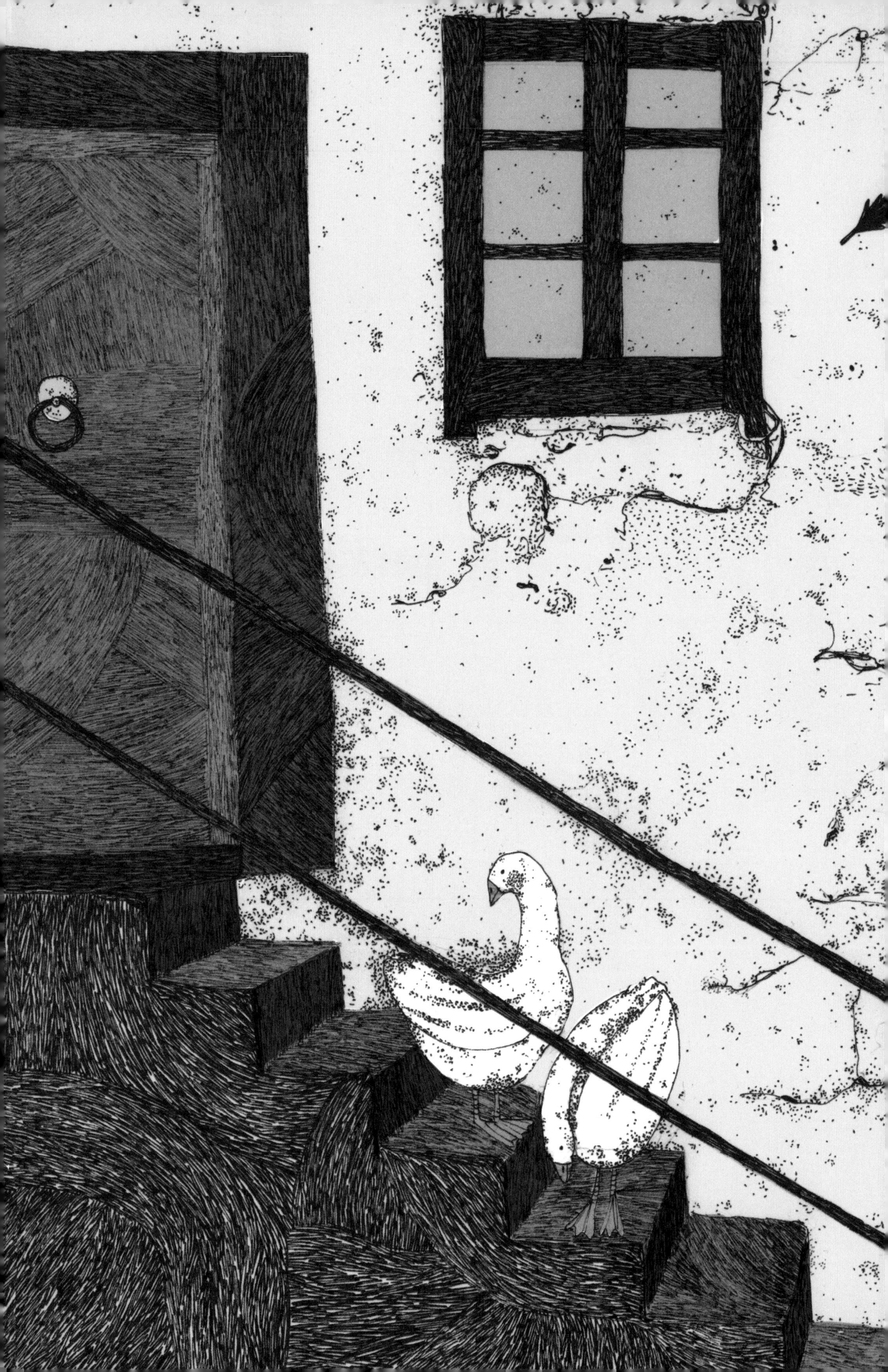

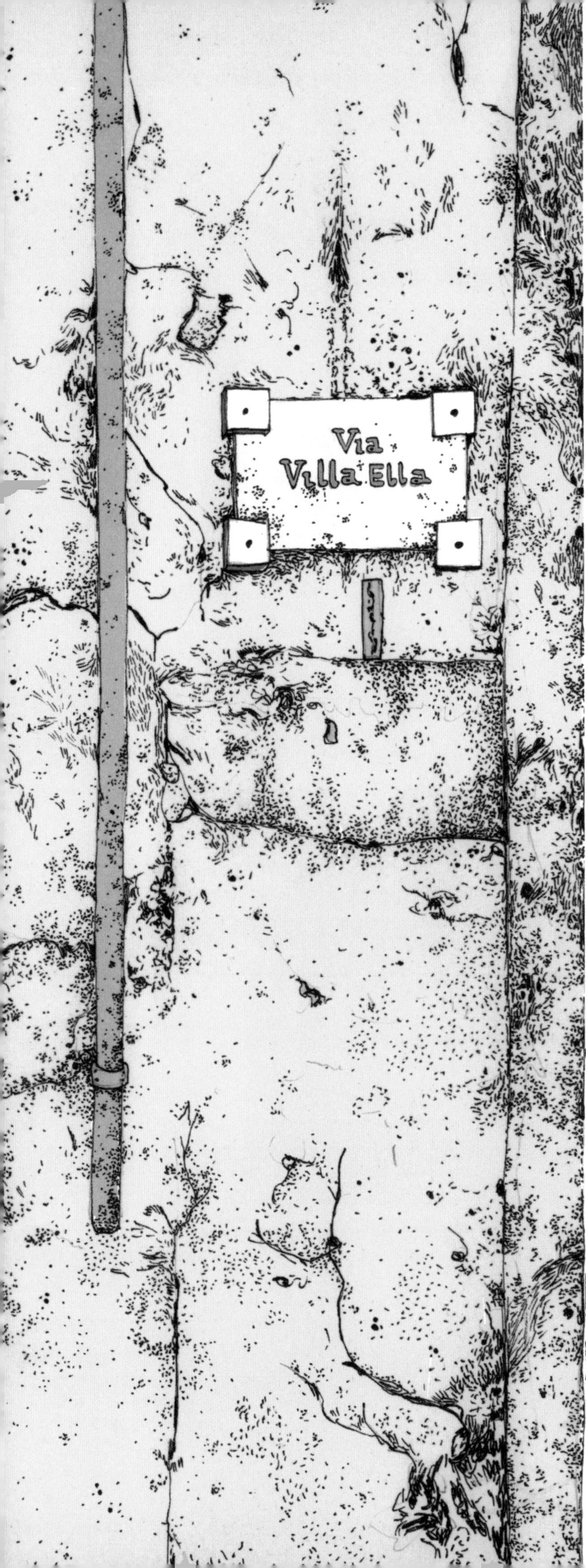
Via
Villa Ella

# LOVE AT FIRST SIGHT

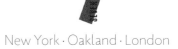

New York · Oakland · London

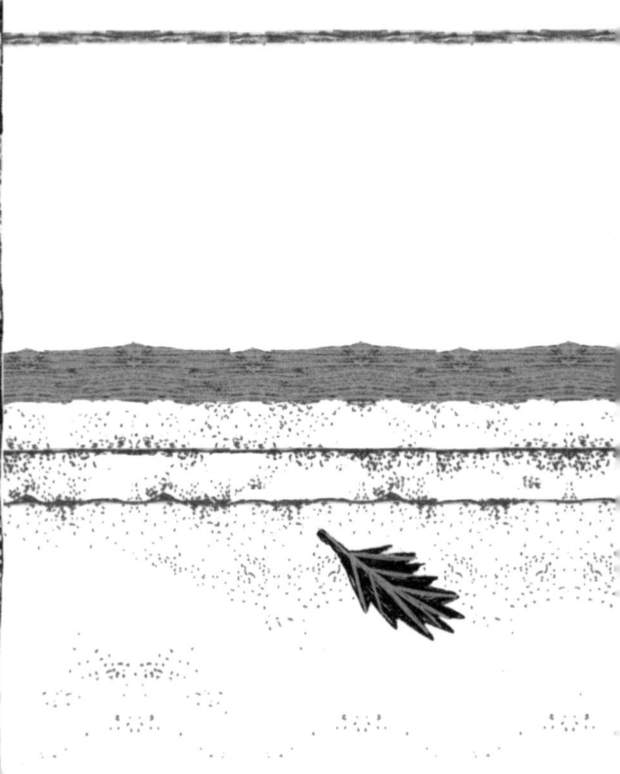

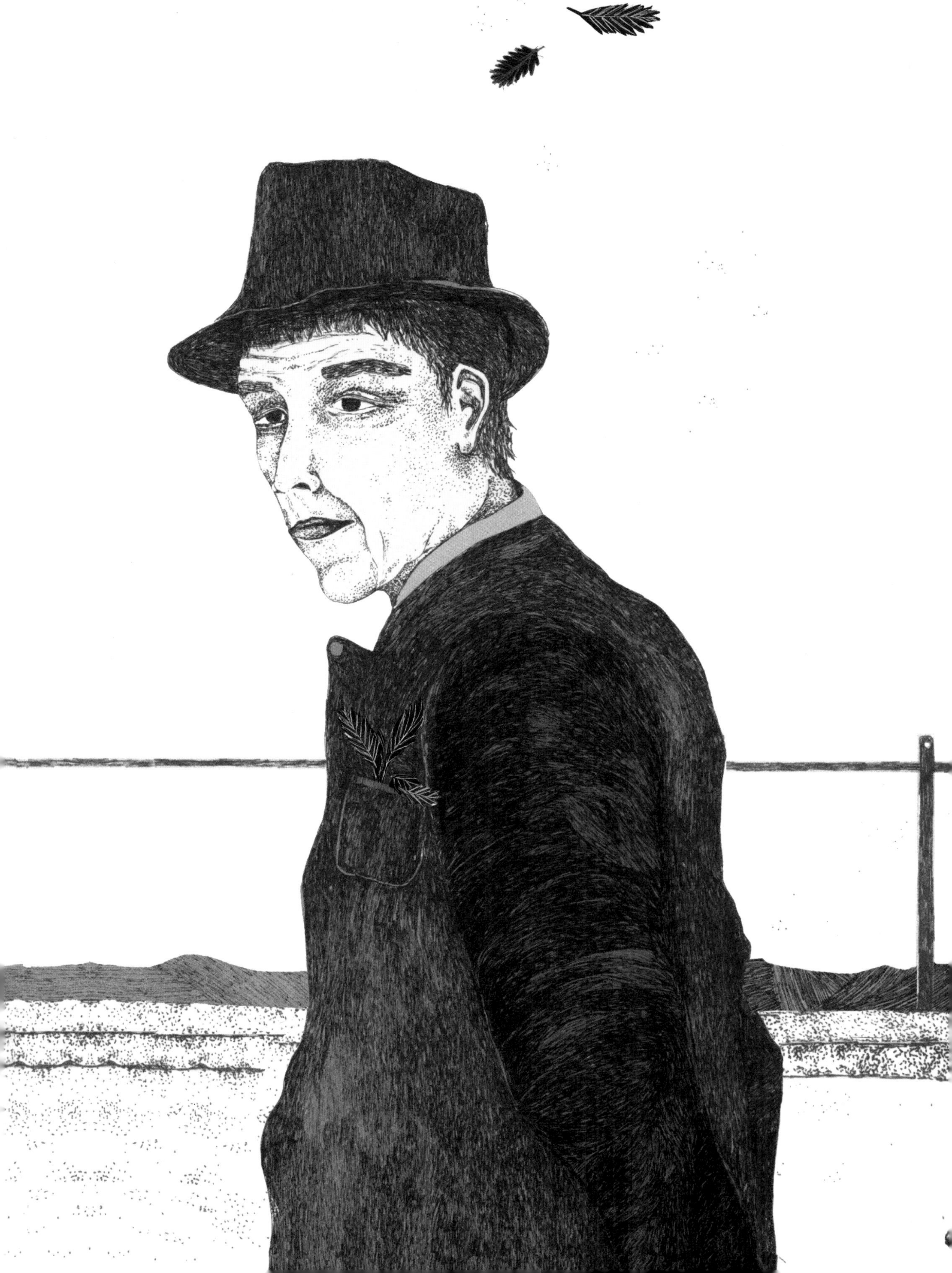

# Love at First Sight

from *Map: Collected and Last Poems*
by Wisława Szymborska,
translated from Polish
by Clare Cavanagh and Stanisław Barańczak,
illustrated by Beatrice Gasca Queirazza

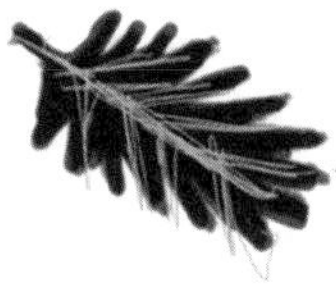

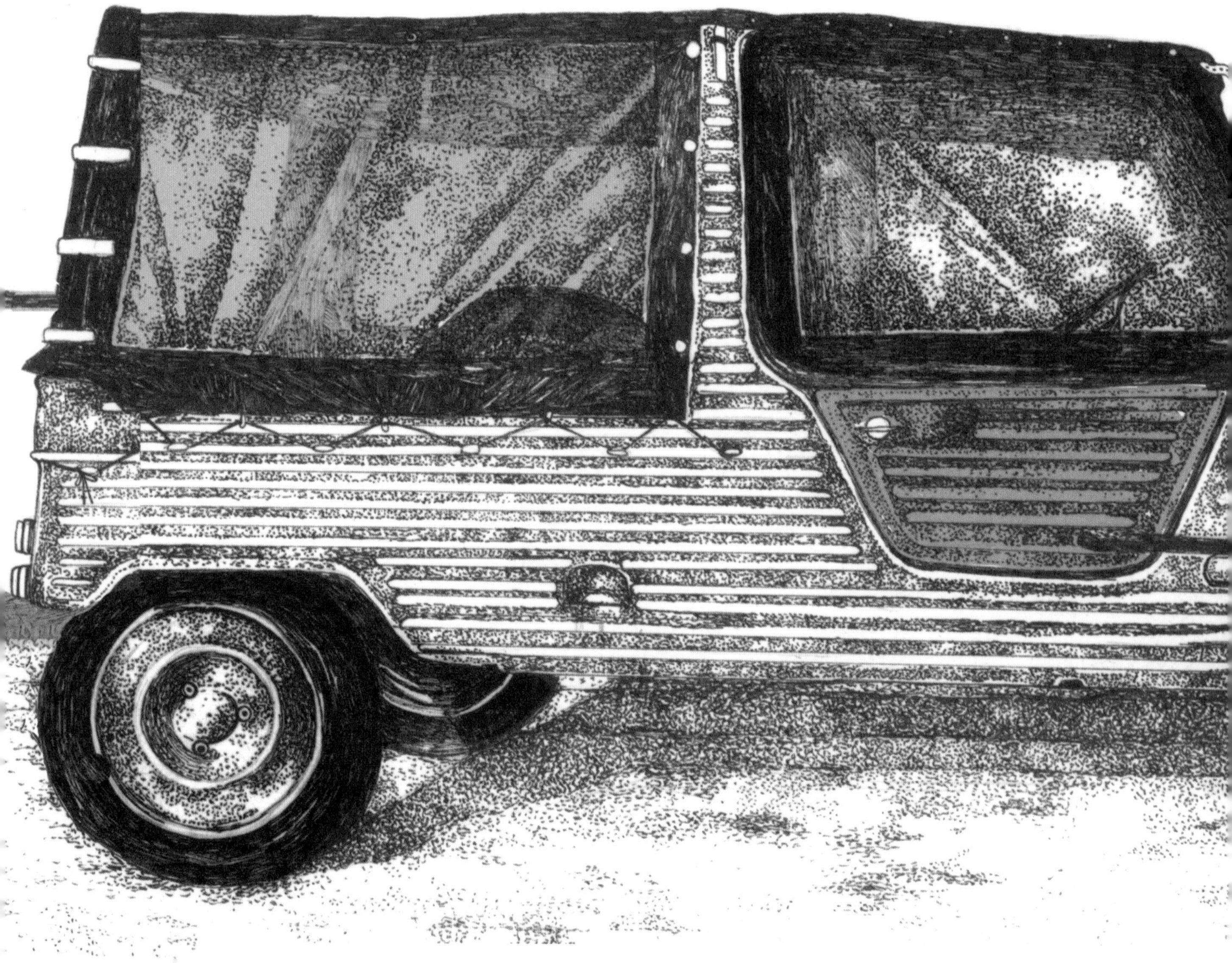

They're both convinced
that a sudden passion joined them.

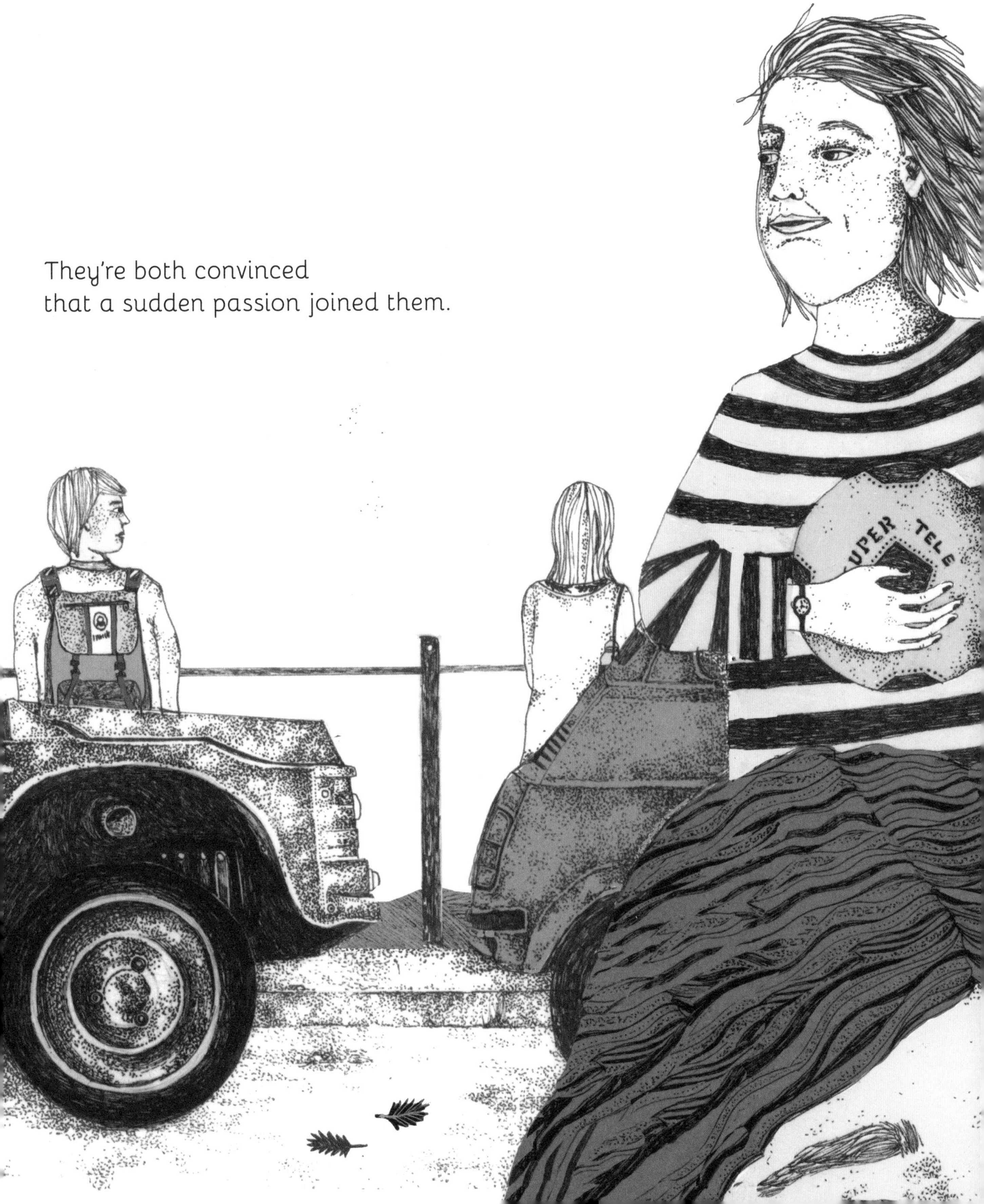
UPER TELE

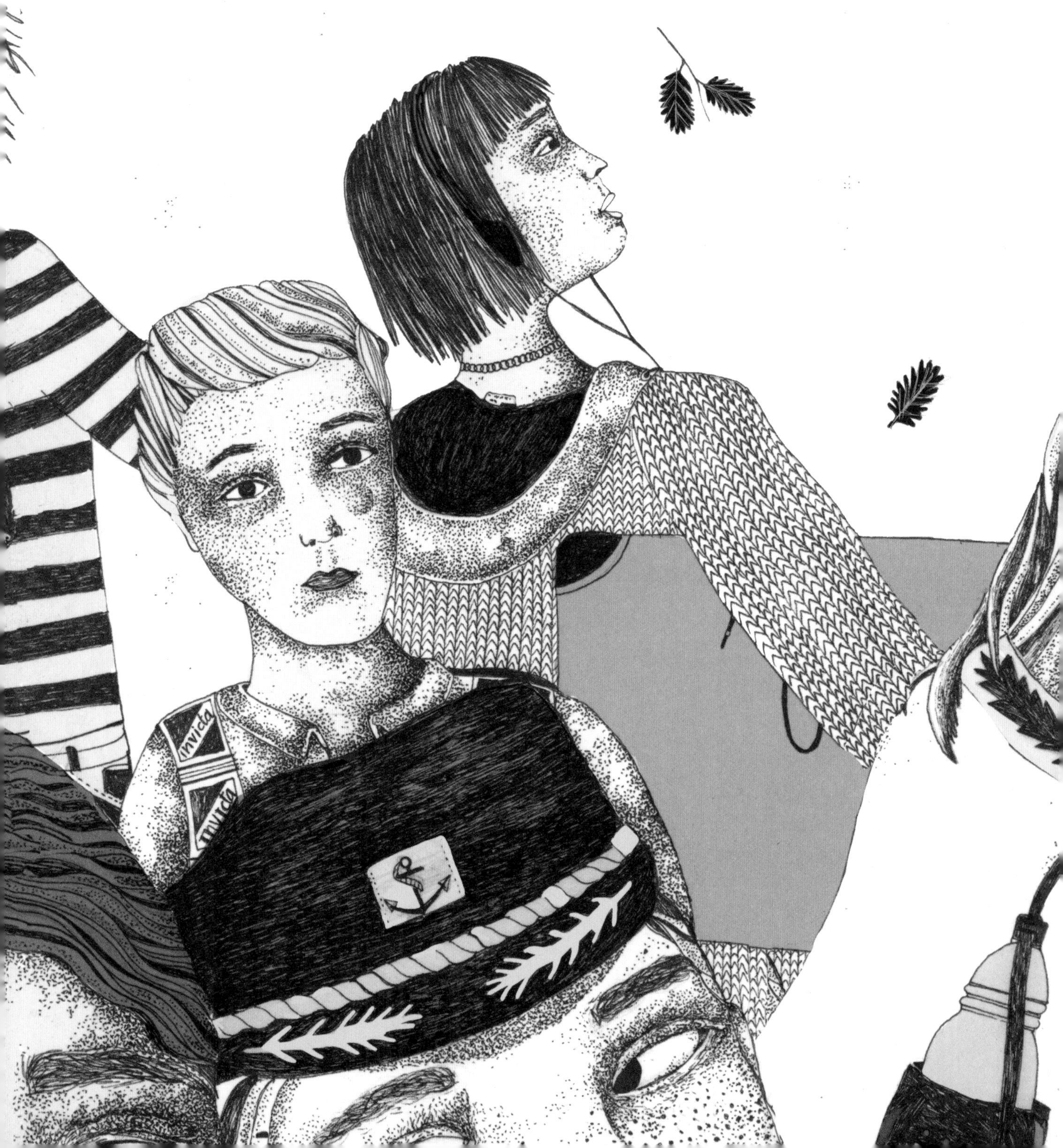
invicta
invicta

Such certainty is beautiful,
but uncertainty is more beautiful still.

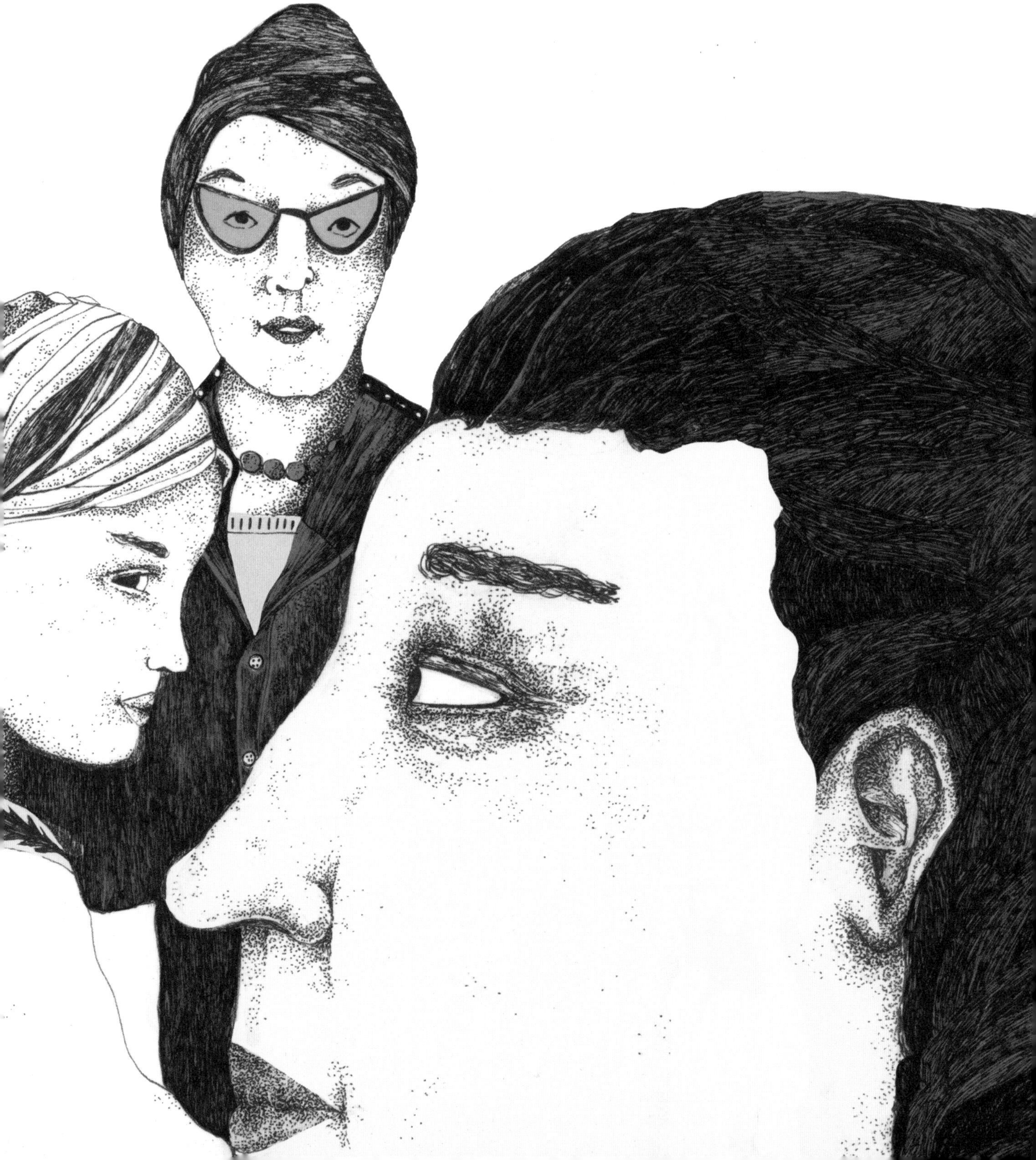

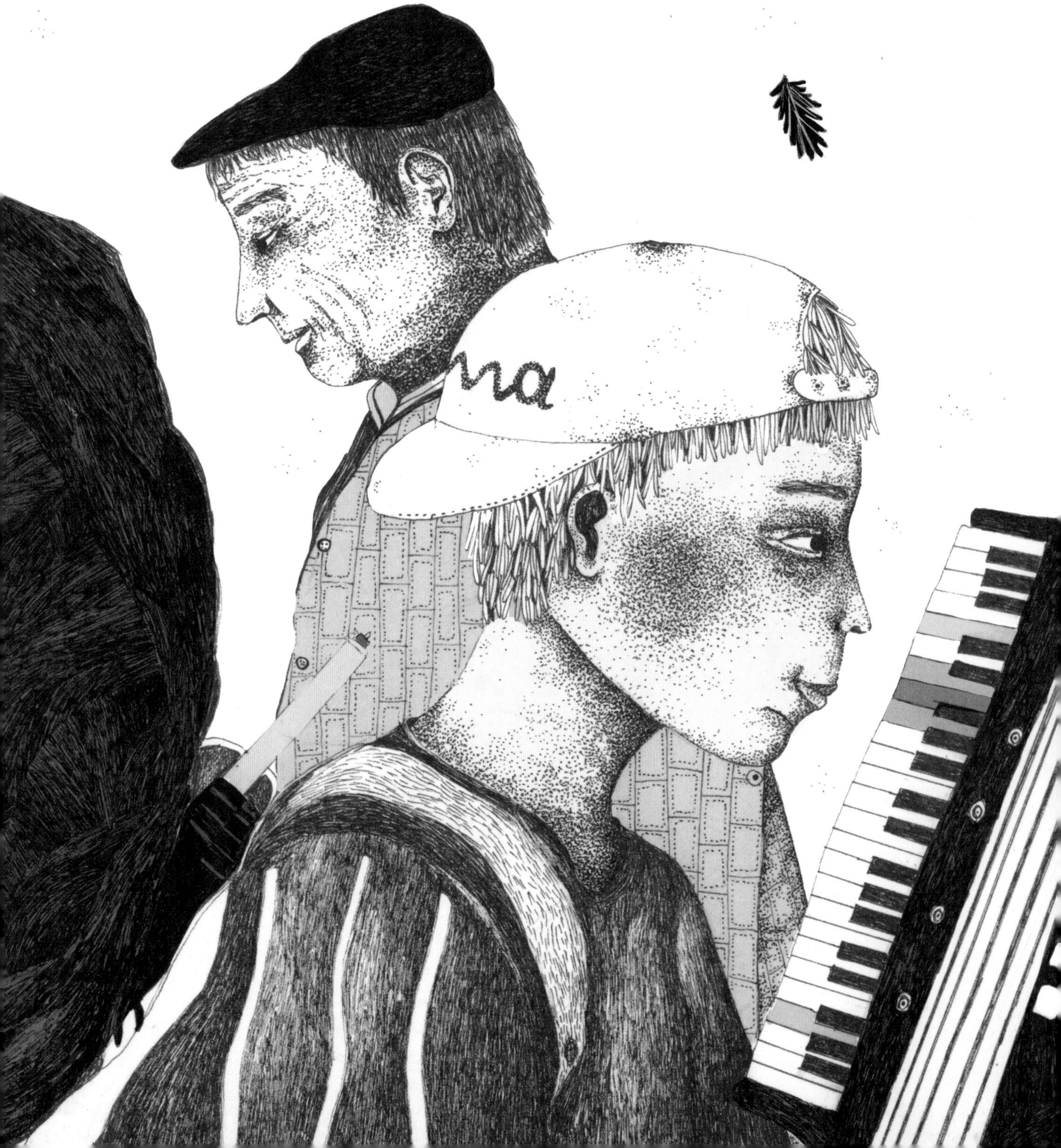
na

Since they'd never met before, they're sure
that there'd been nothing between them.
But what's the word from the streets, staircases, hallways—
perhaps they've passed by each other a million times?

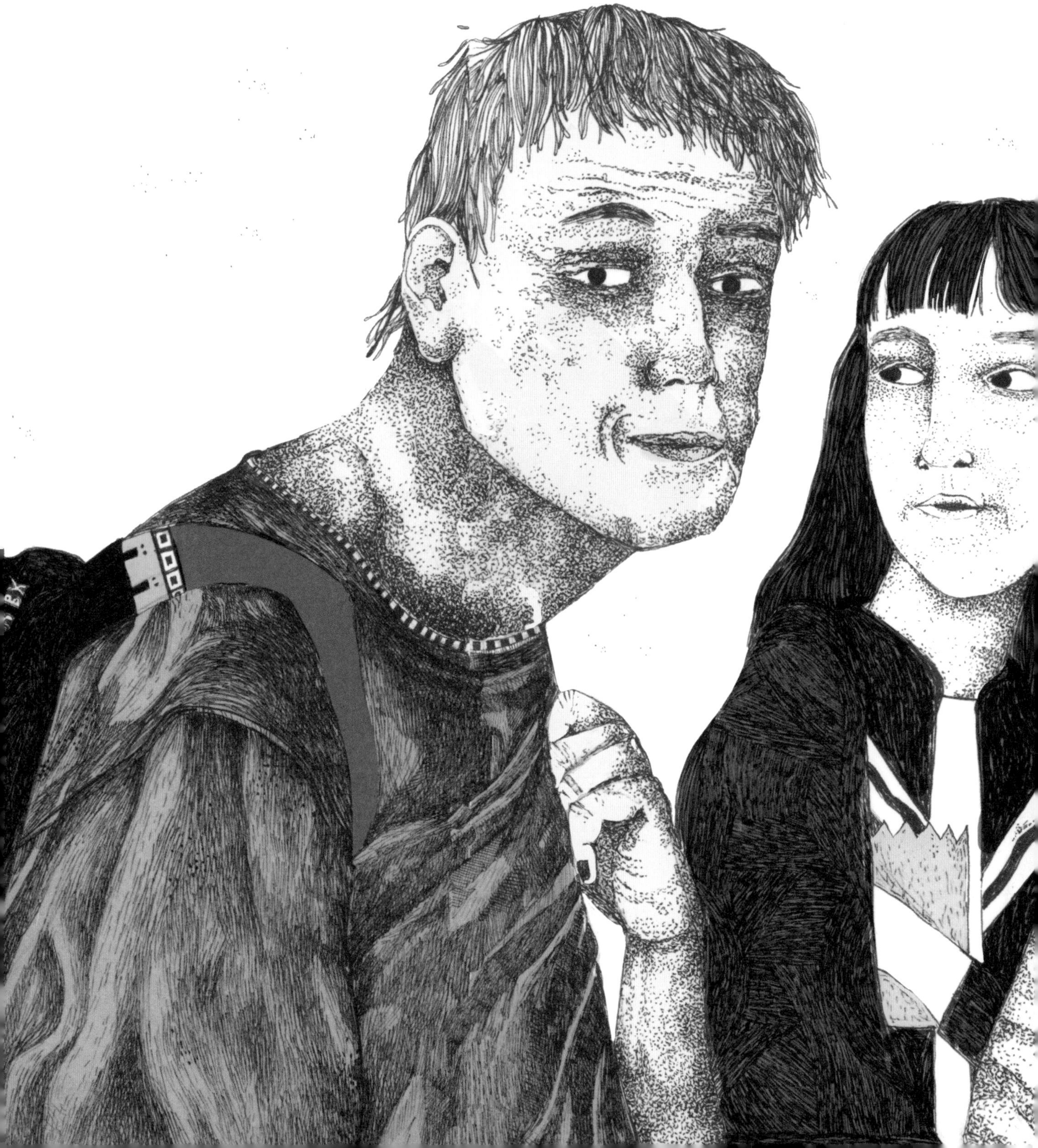

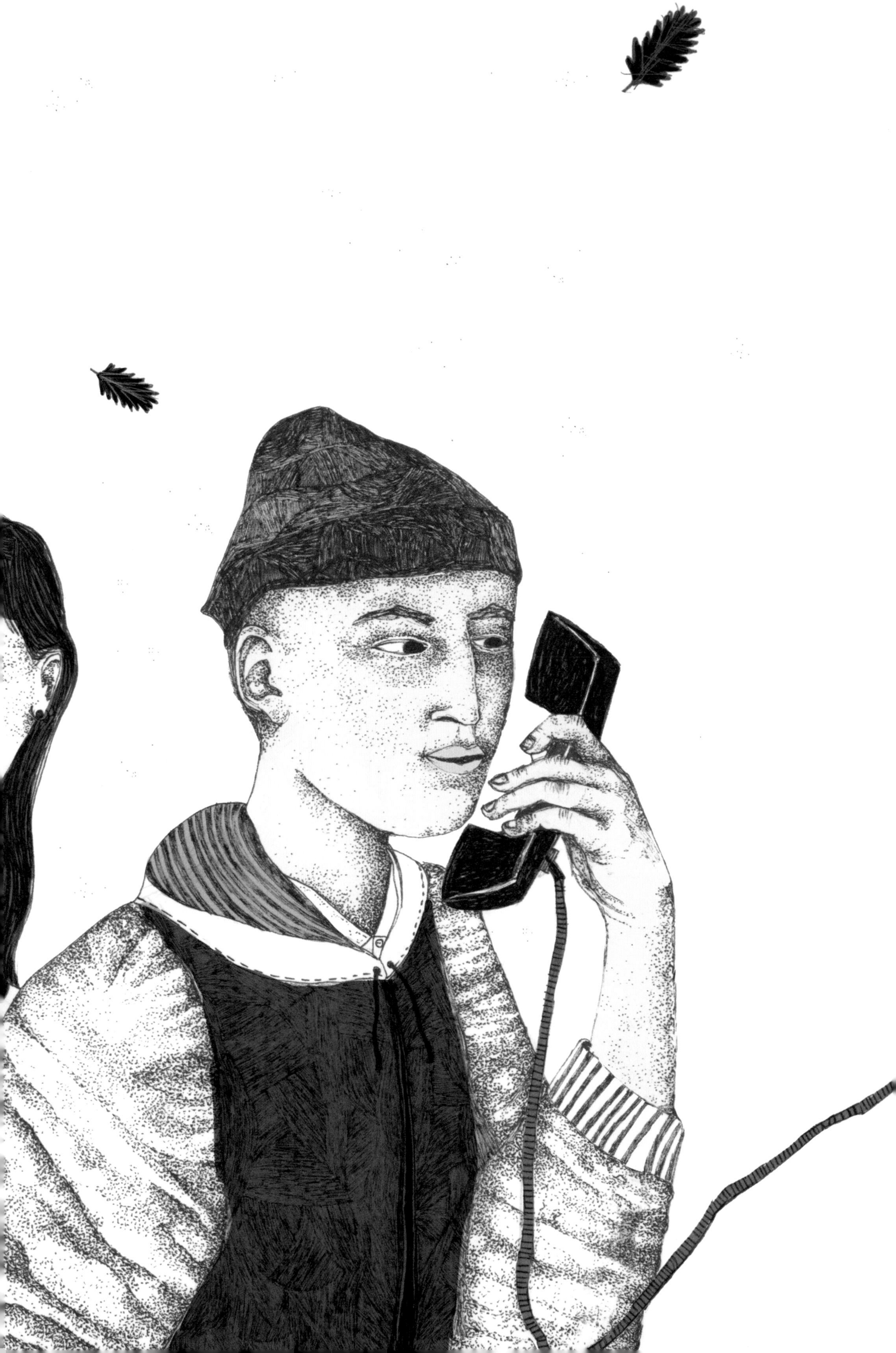

I want to ask them
if they don't remember—
a moment face to face
in some revolving door?
perhaps a "sorry" muttered in a crowd?
a curt "wrong number" caught in the receiver?—

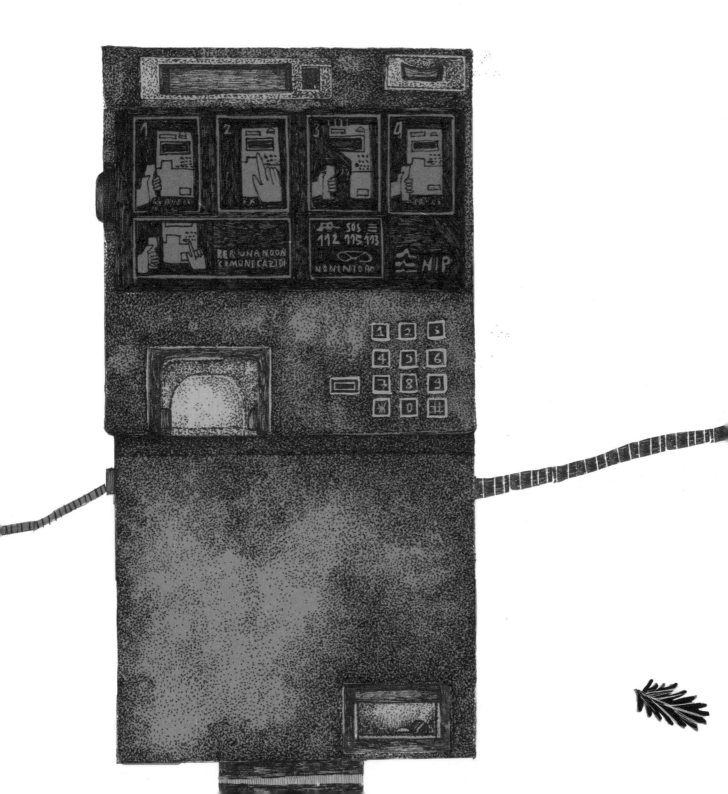

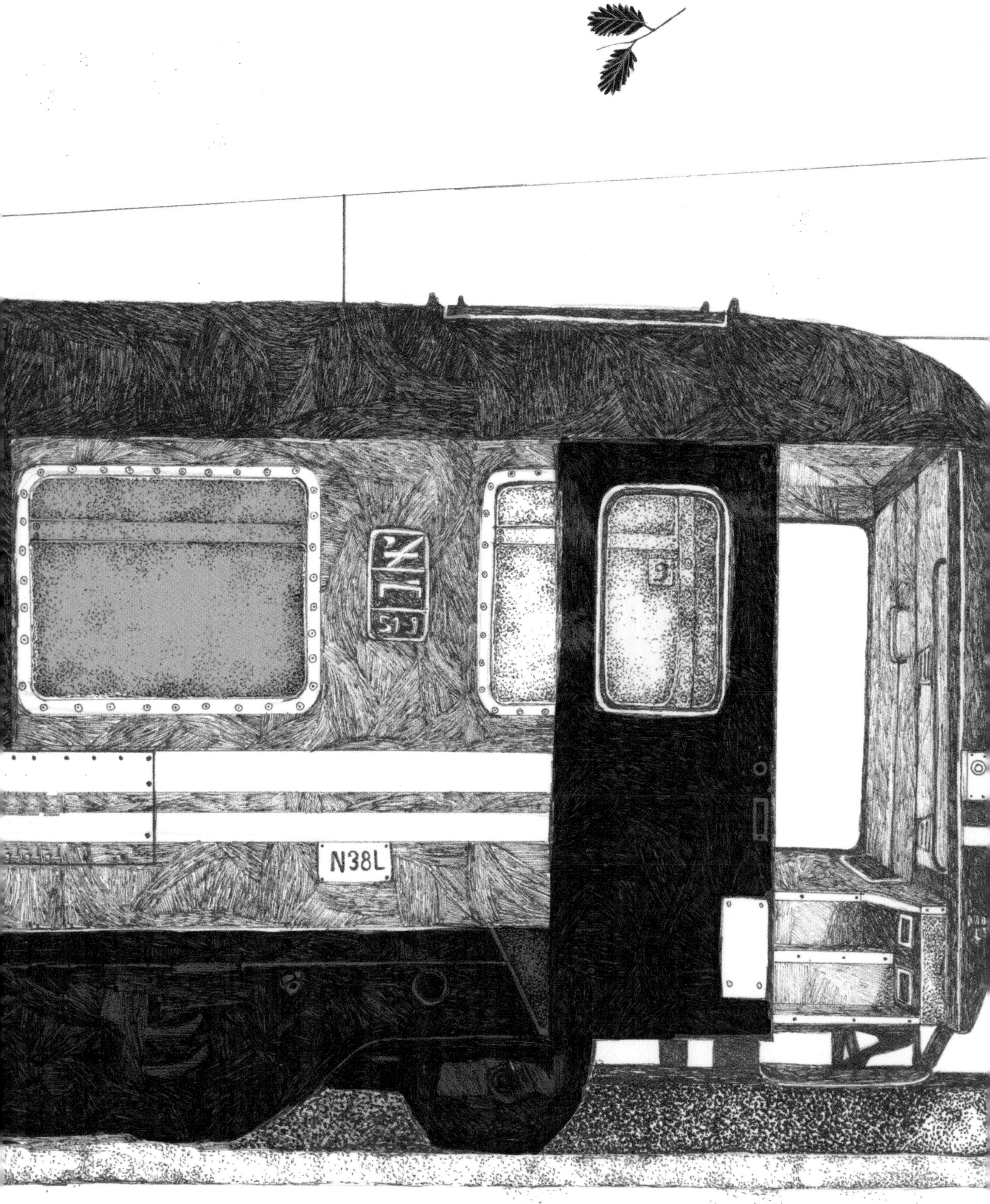
N38L

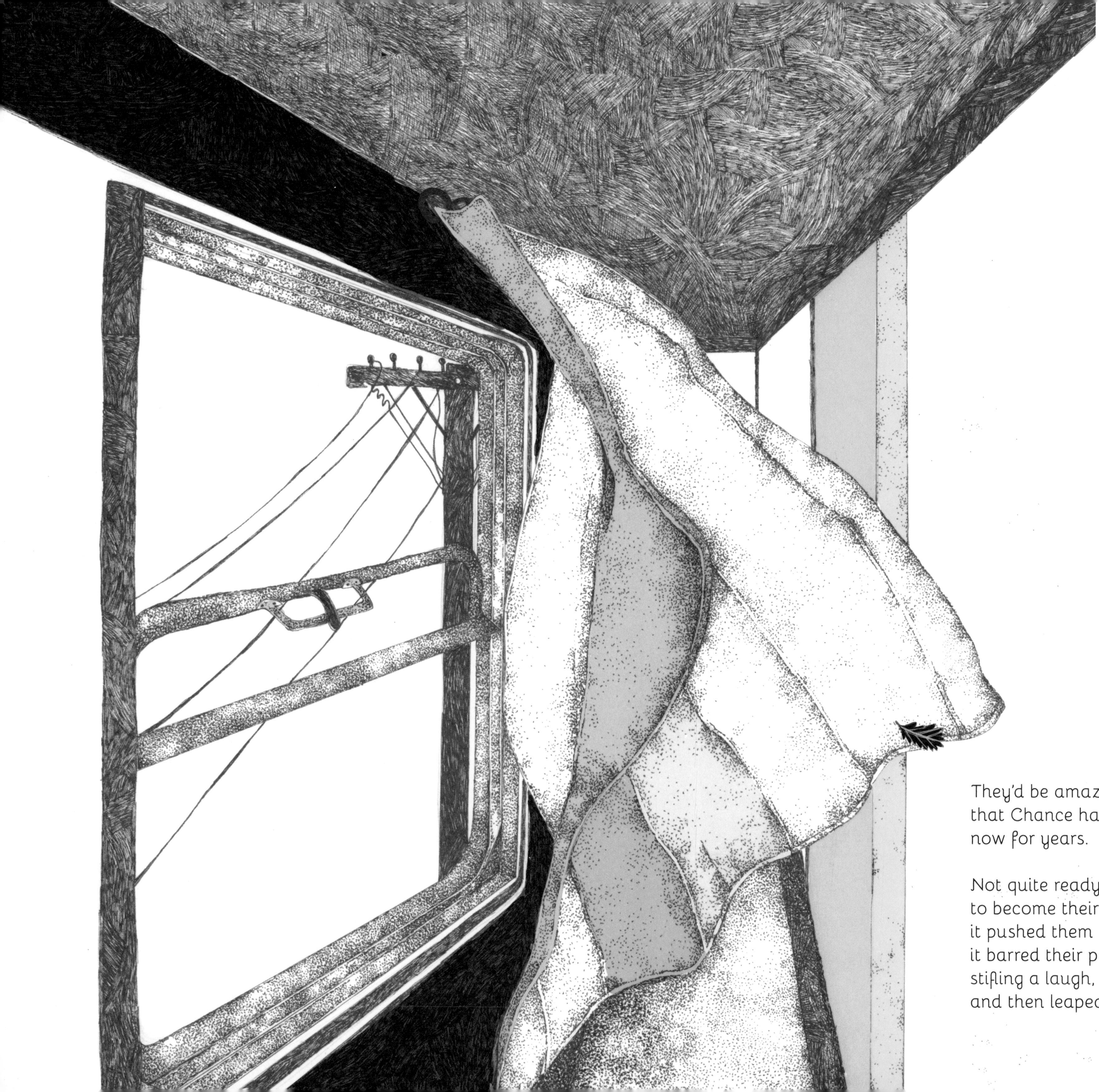

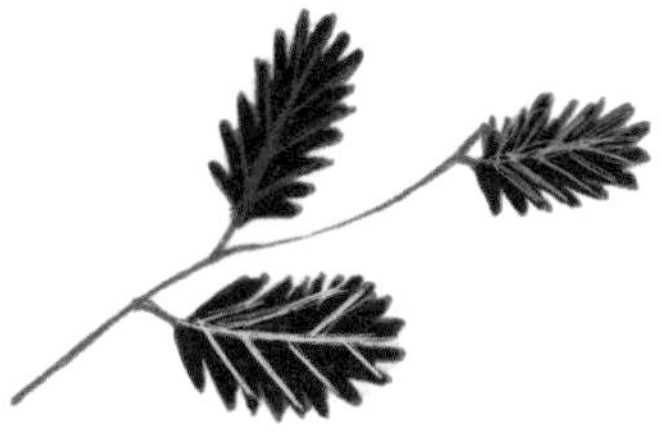

They'd be amazed to hear
that Chance has been toying with them
now for years.

Not quite ready yet
to become their Destiny,
it pushed them close, drove them apart,
it barred their path,
stifling a laugh,
and then leaped aside.

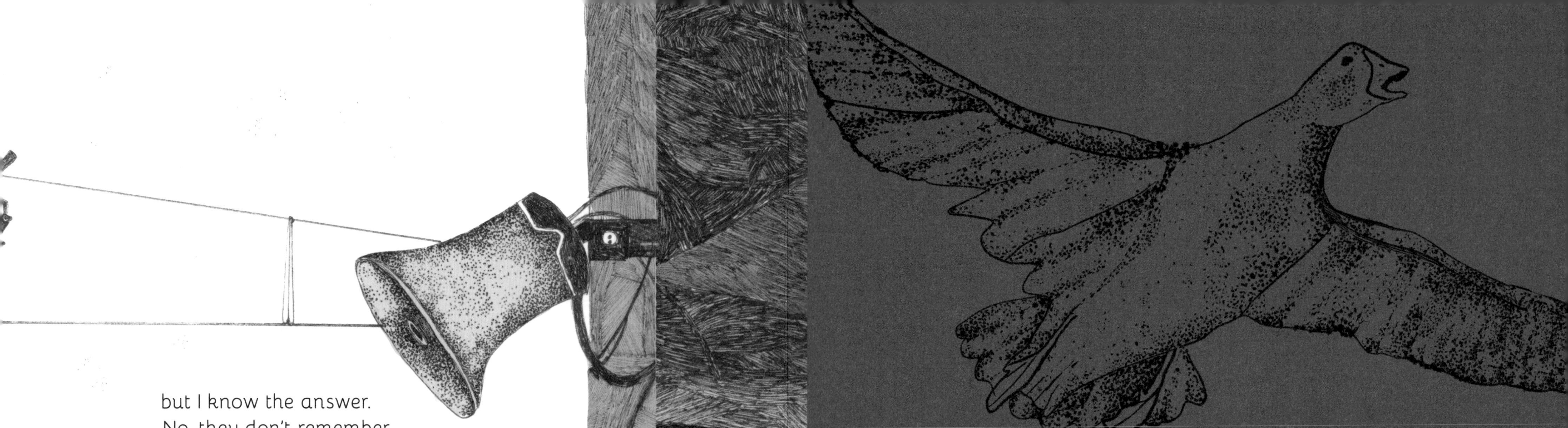

but I know the answer.
No, they don't remember.

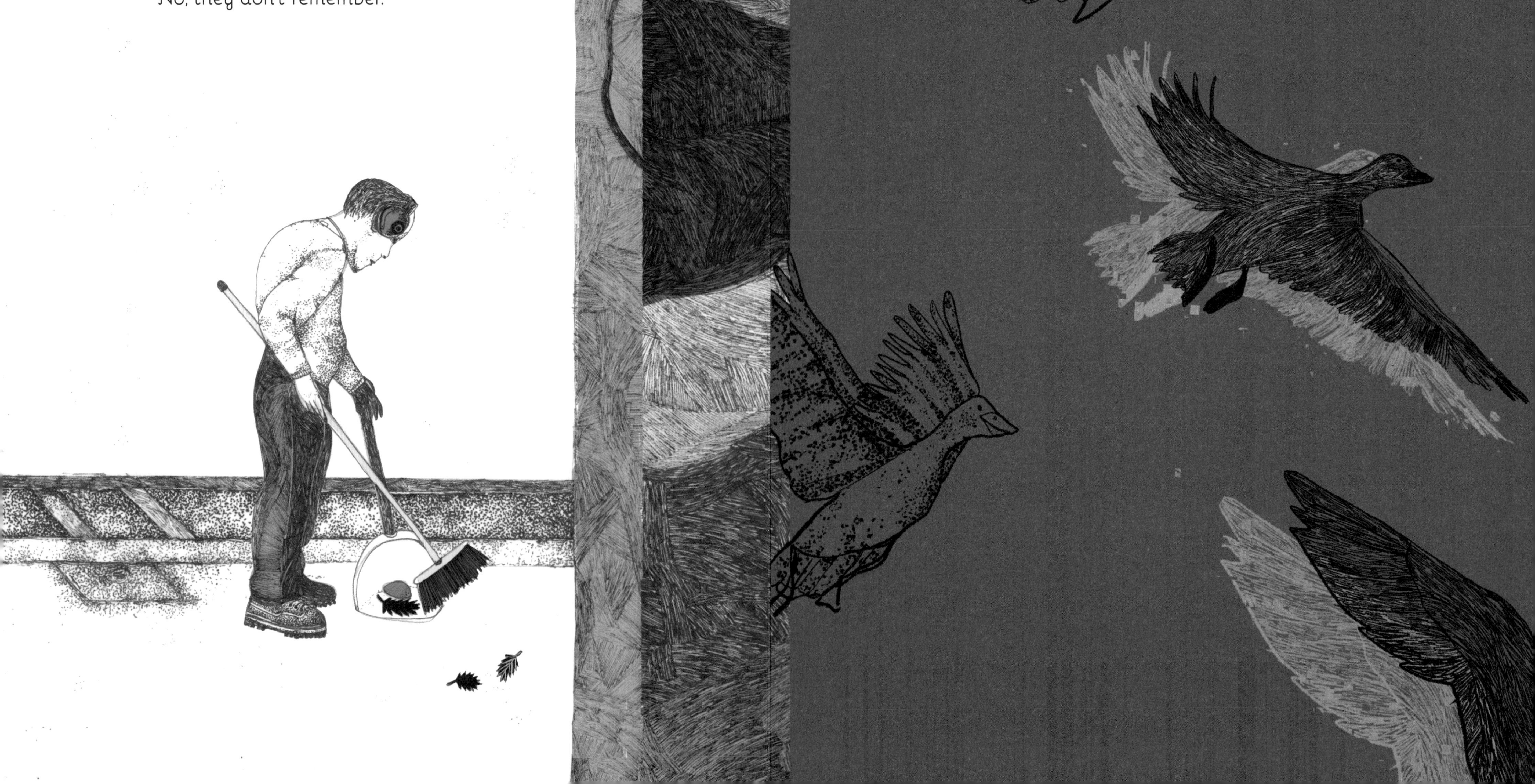

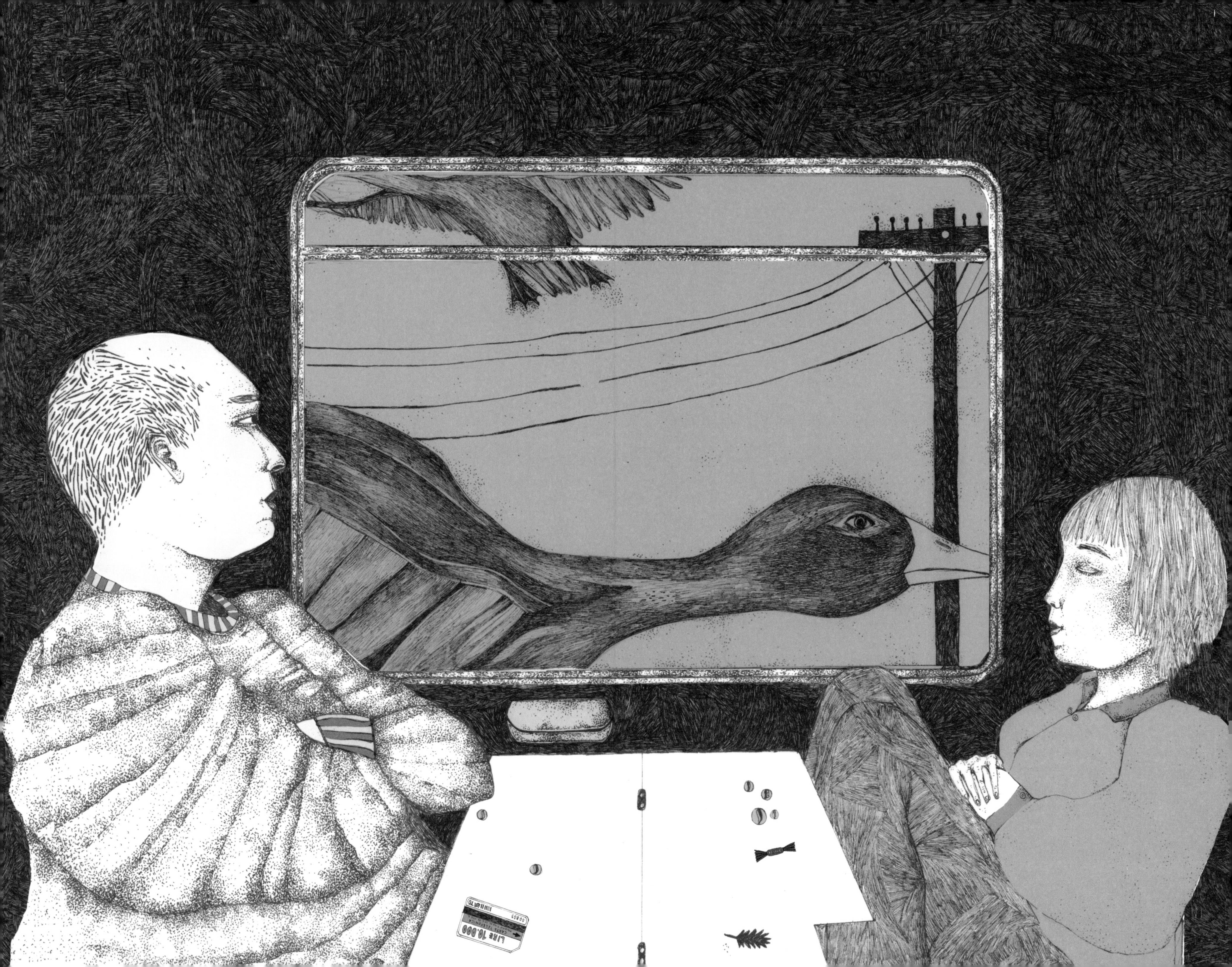
LIRE 10.000

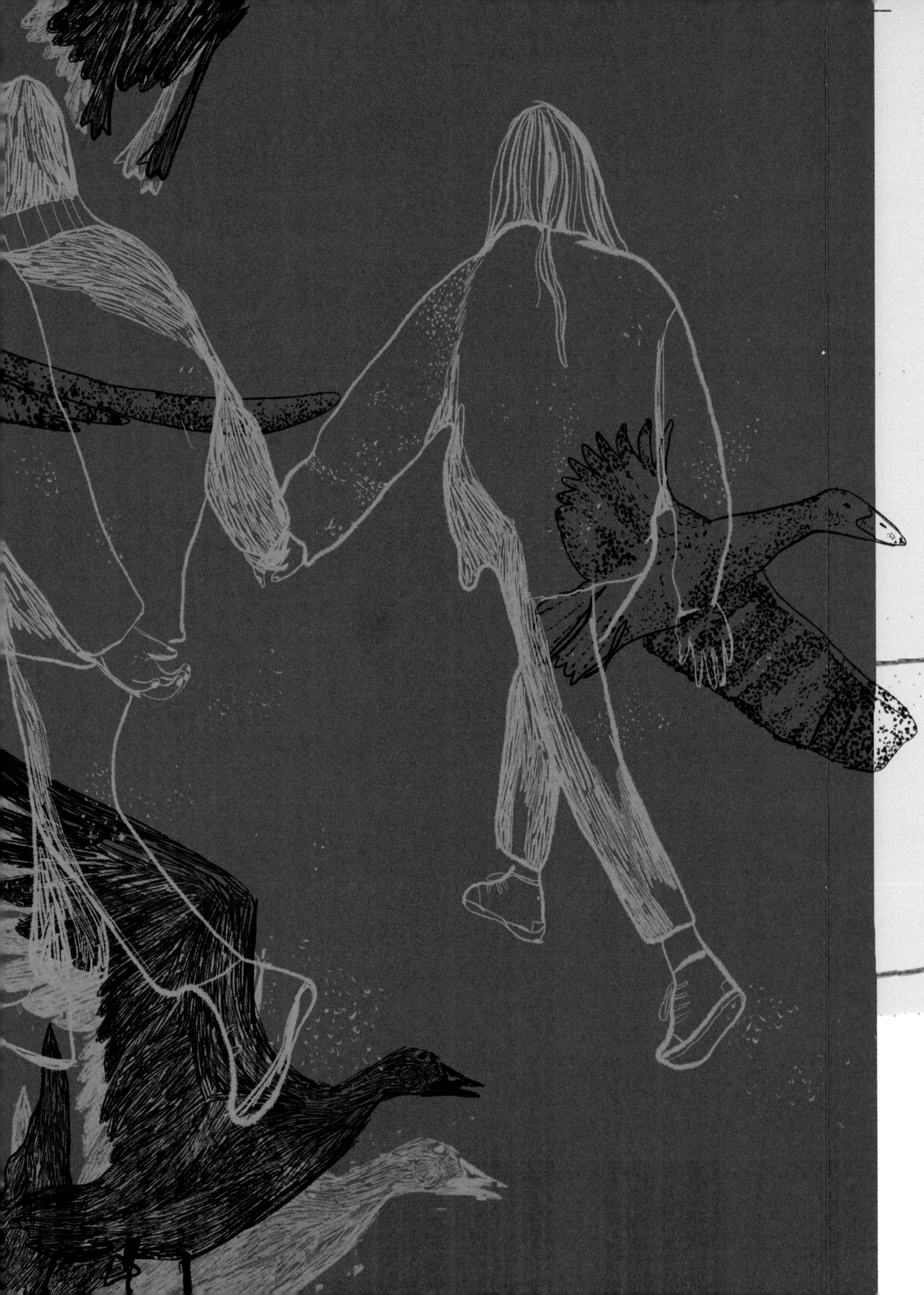

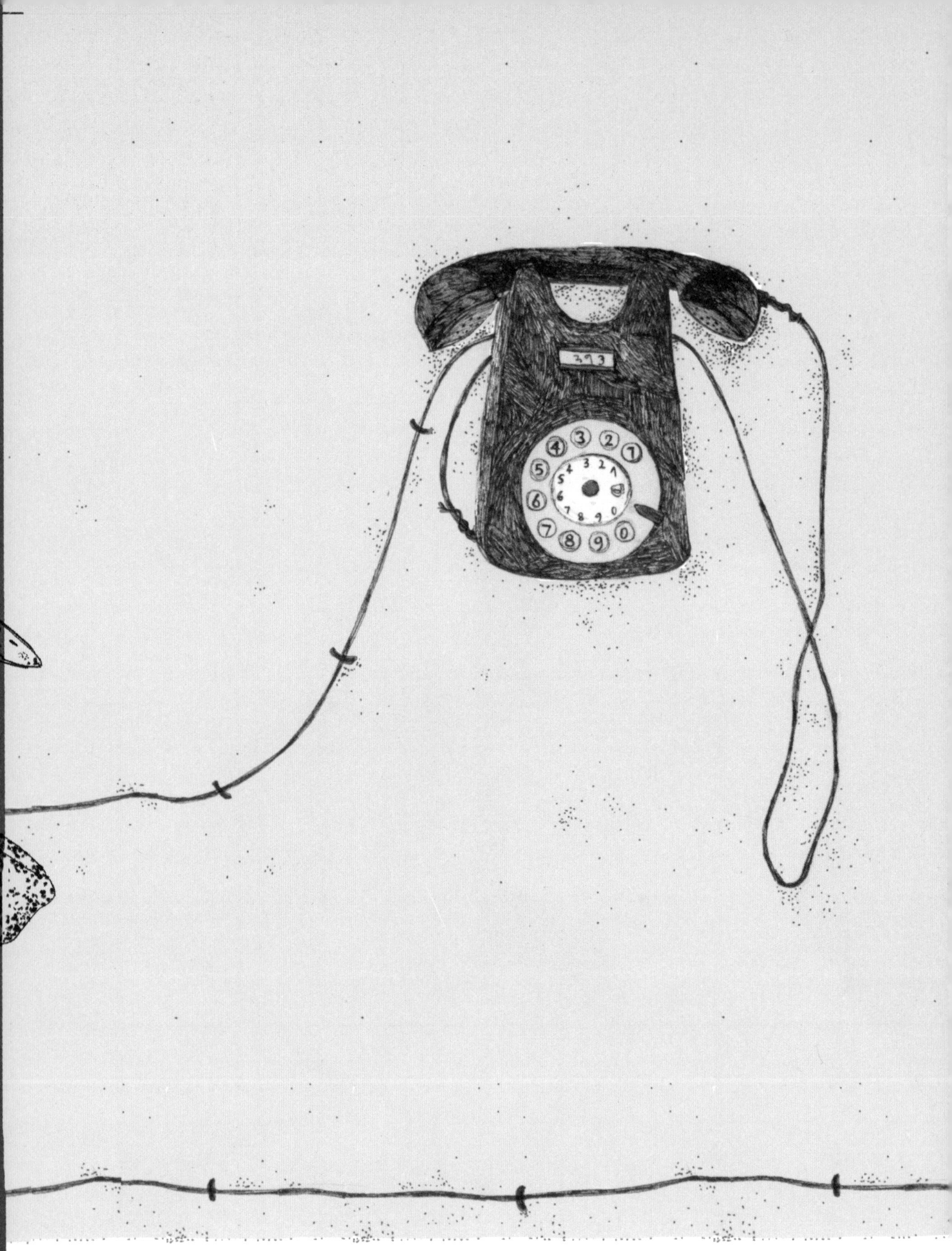

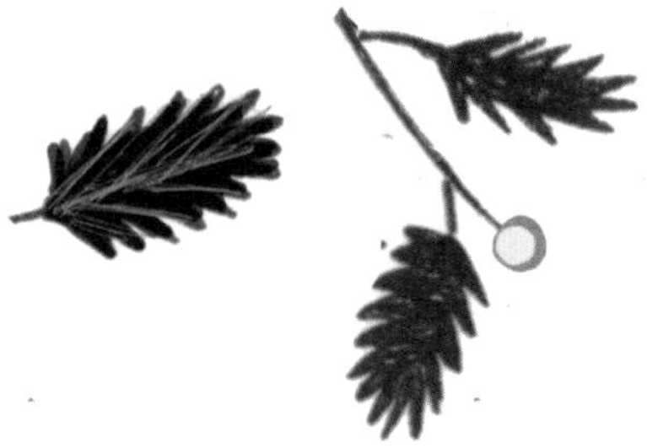

There were signs and signals,
even if they couldn't read them yet.

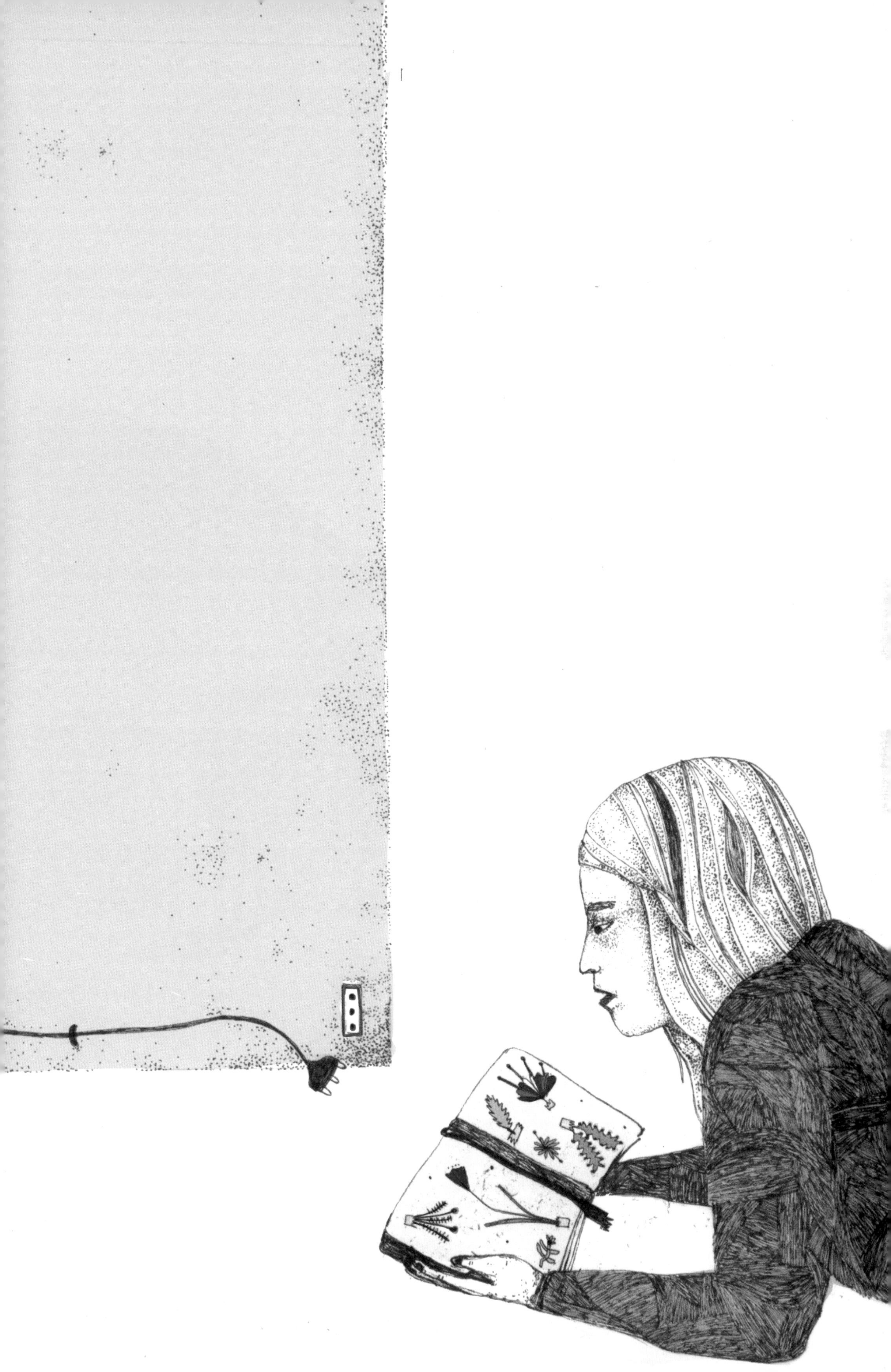

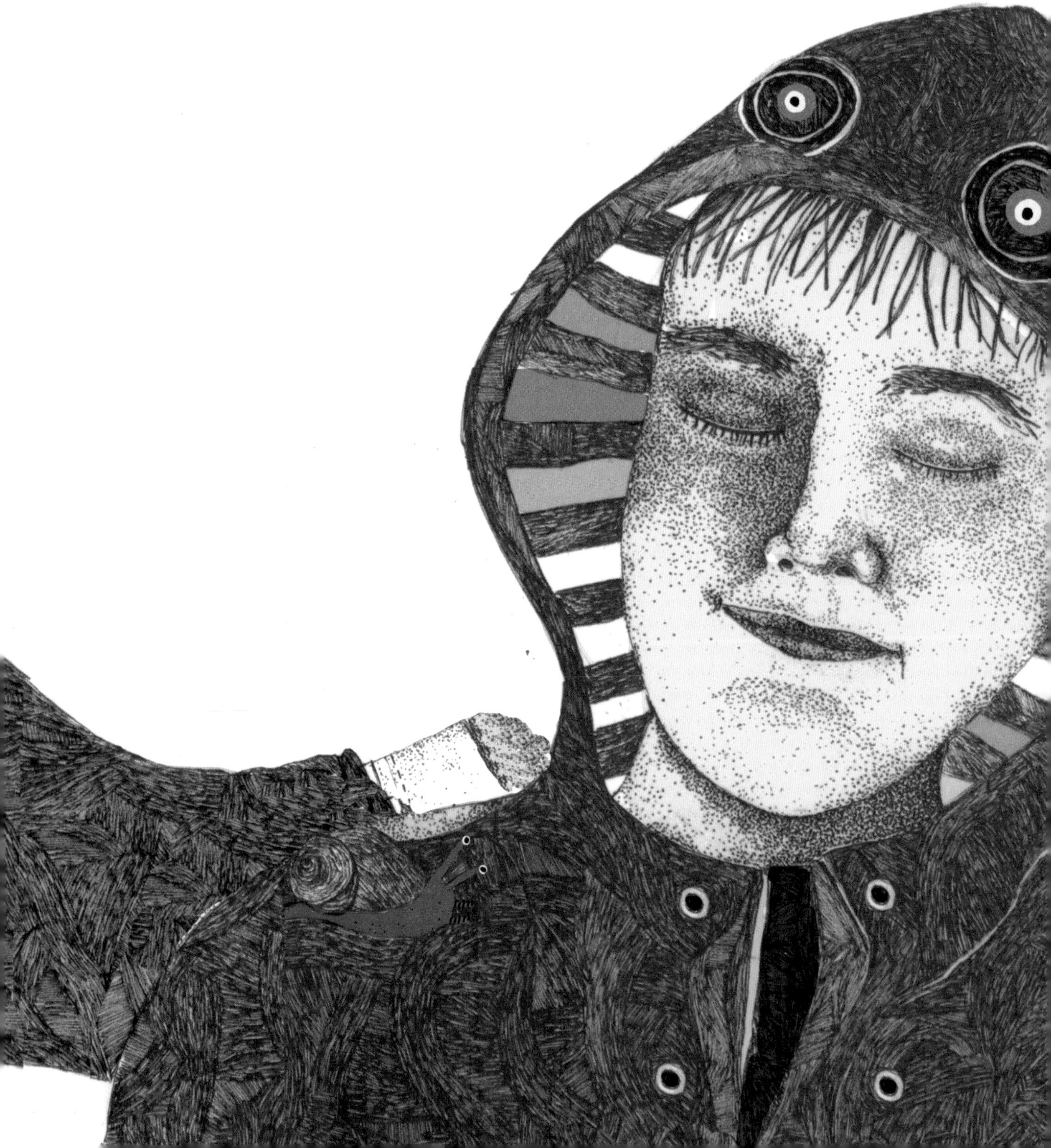

Perhaps three years ago
or just last Tuesday
a certain leaf fluttered
from one shoulder to another?
Something was dropped and then picked up.

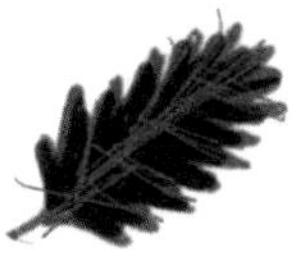

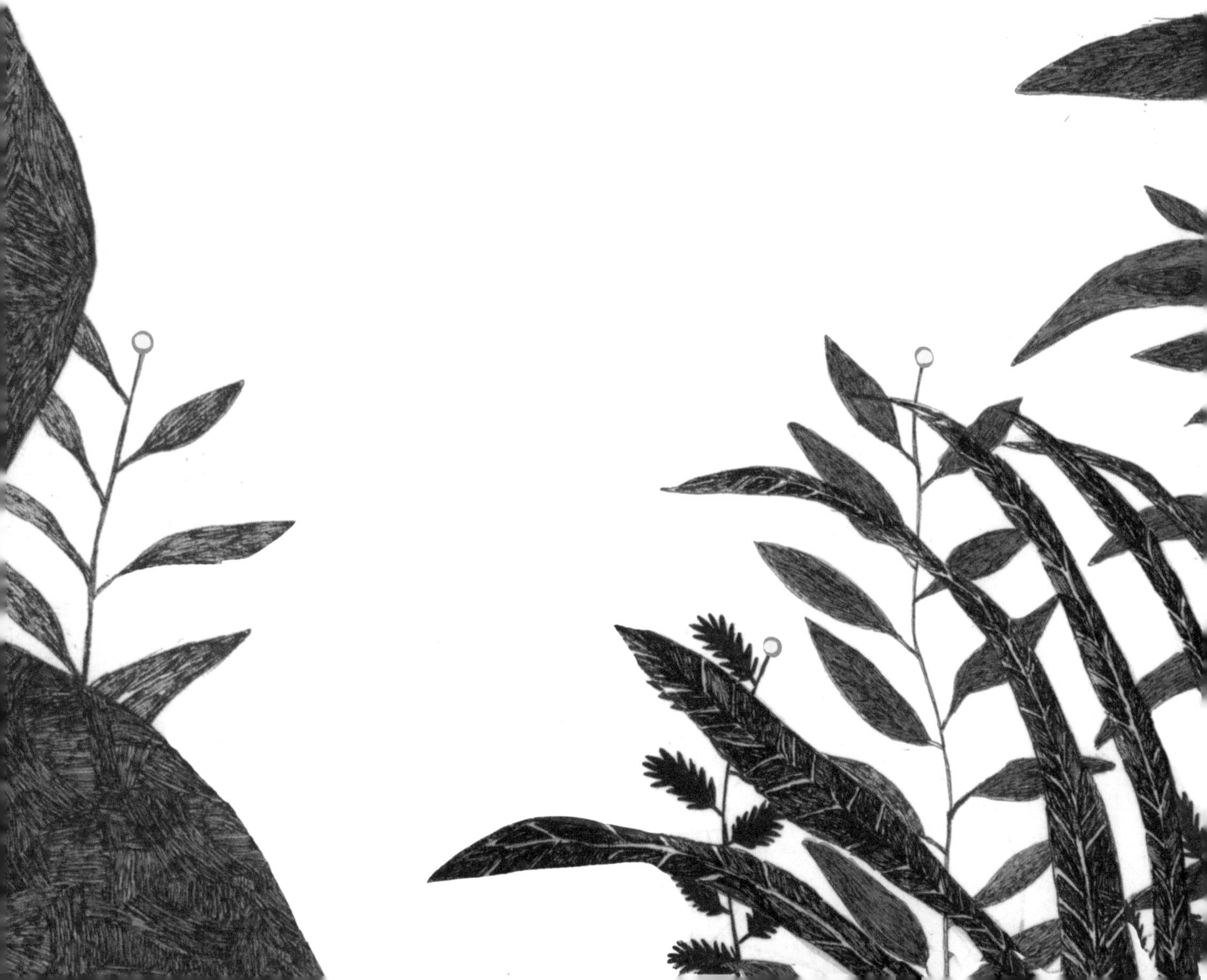

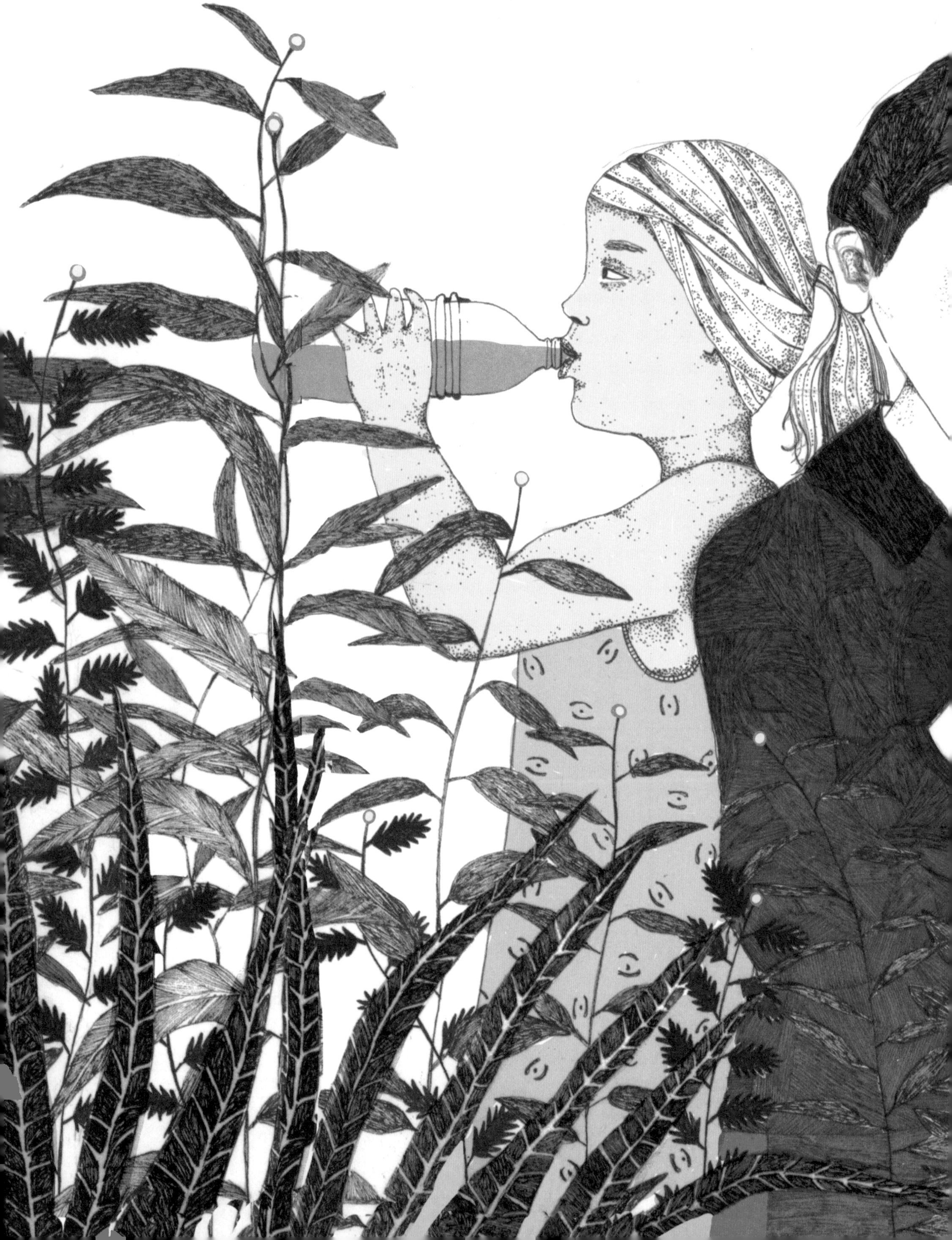

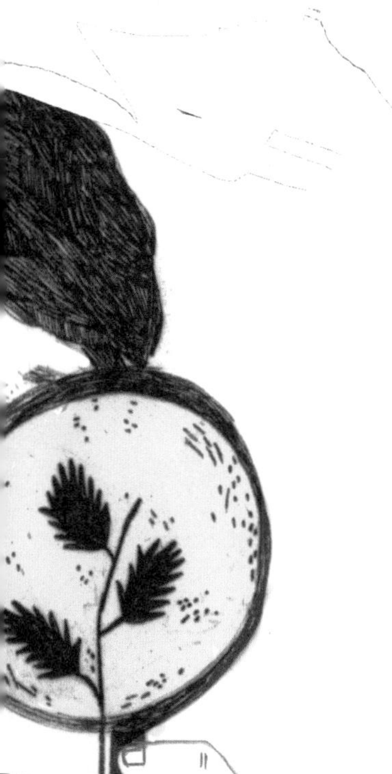

Who knows, maybe the ball that vanished
into childhood's thicket?

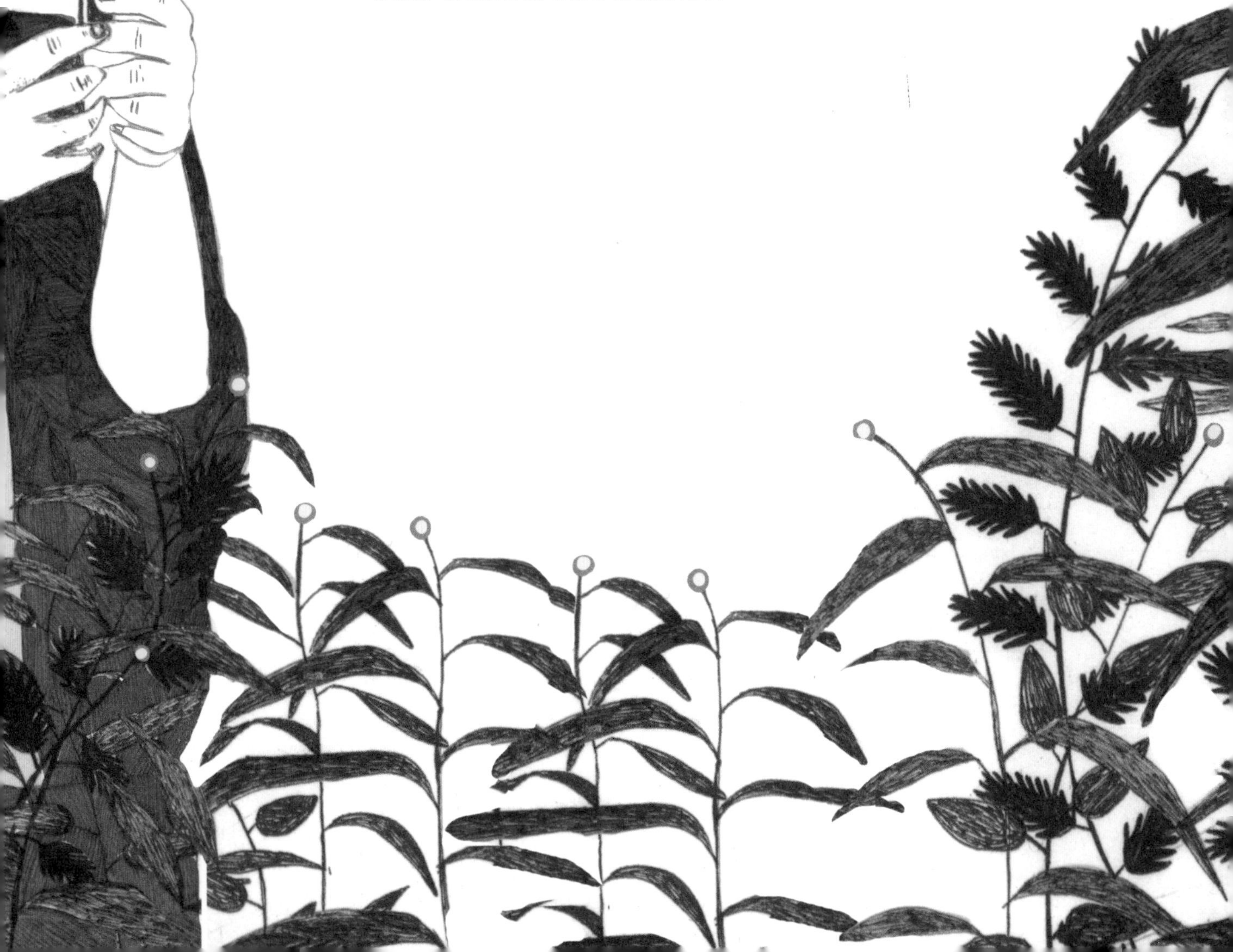

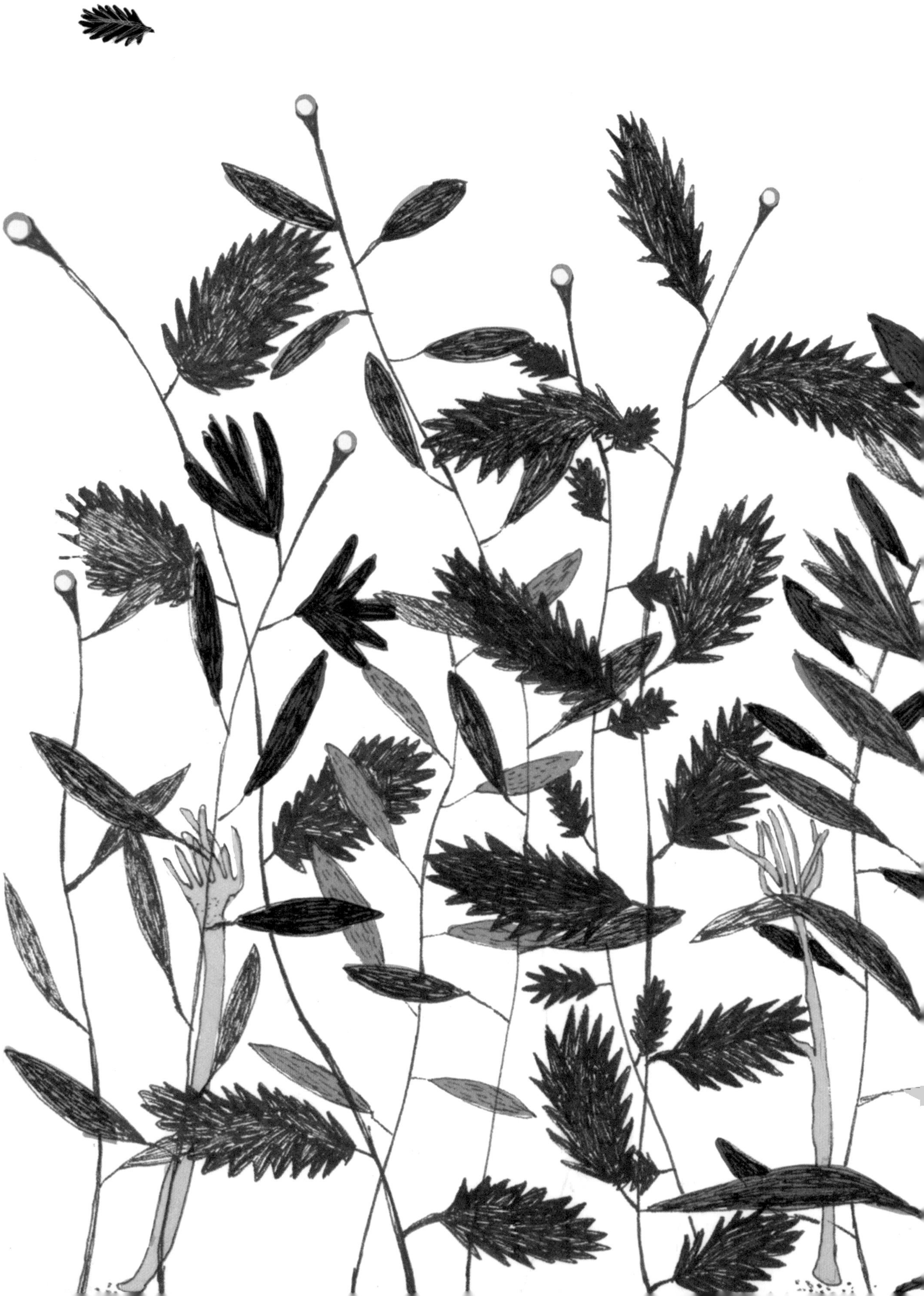

There were doorknobs and doorbells
where one touch had covered another
beforehand.
Suitcases checked and standing side by side.

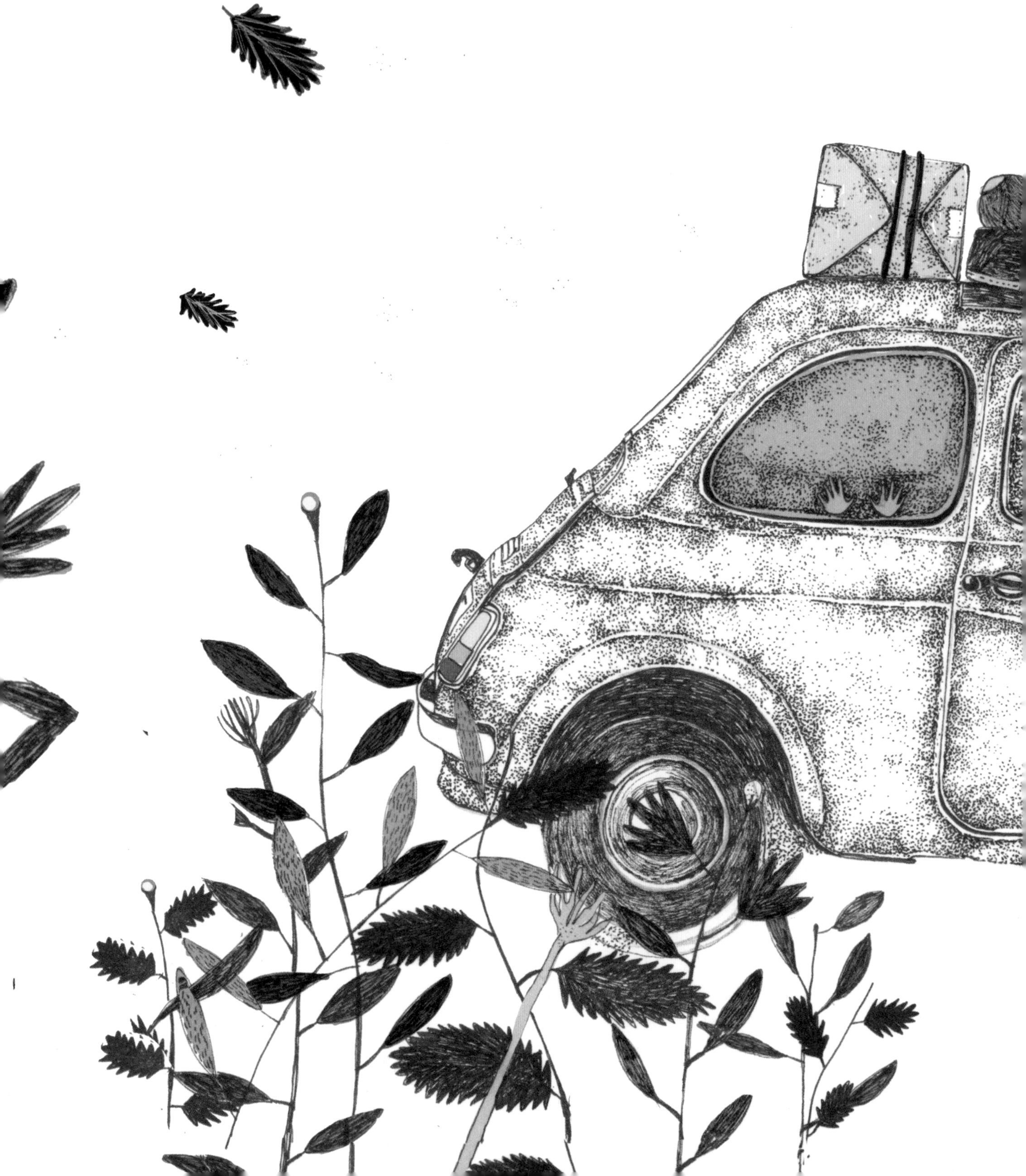

One night, perhaps, the same dream,
grown hazy by morning.

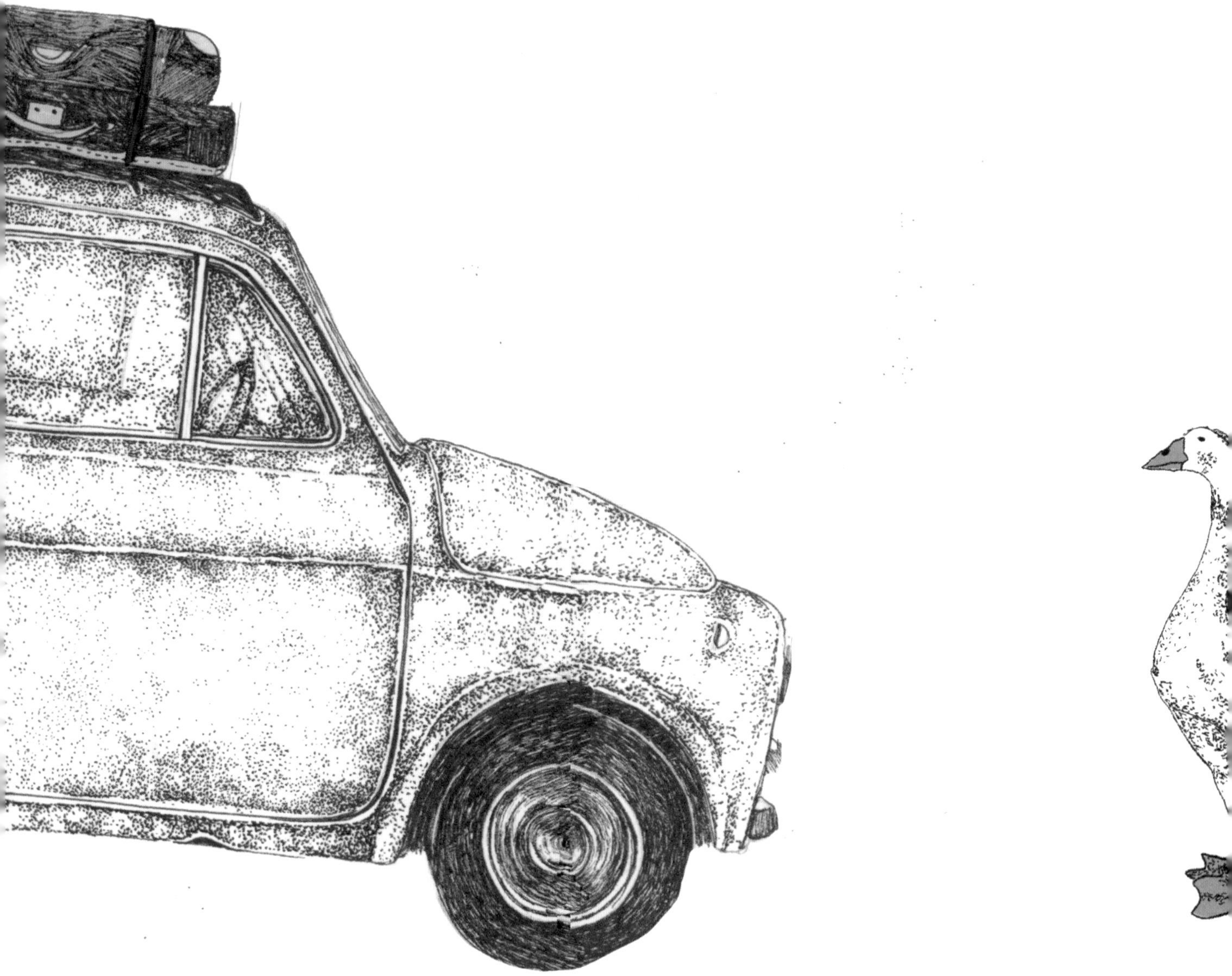

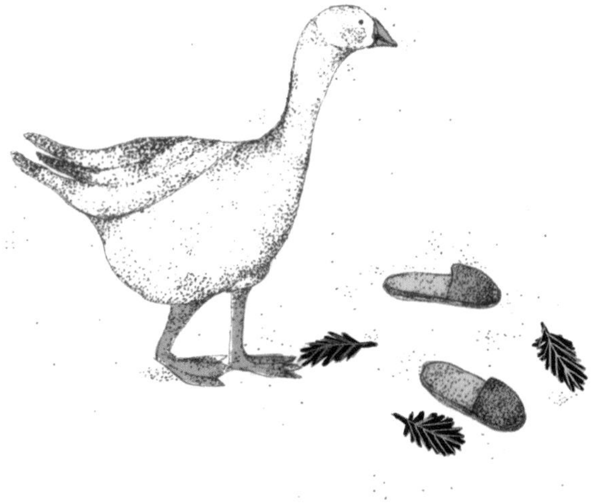

Every beginning
is only a sequel, after all,
and the book of events
is always open halfway through.

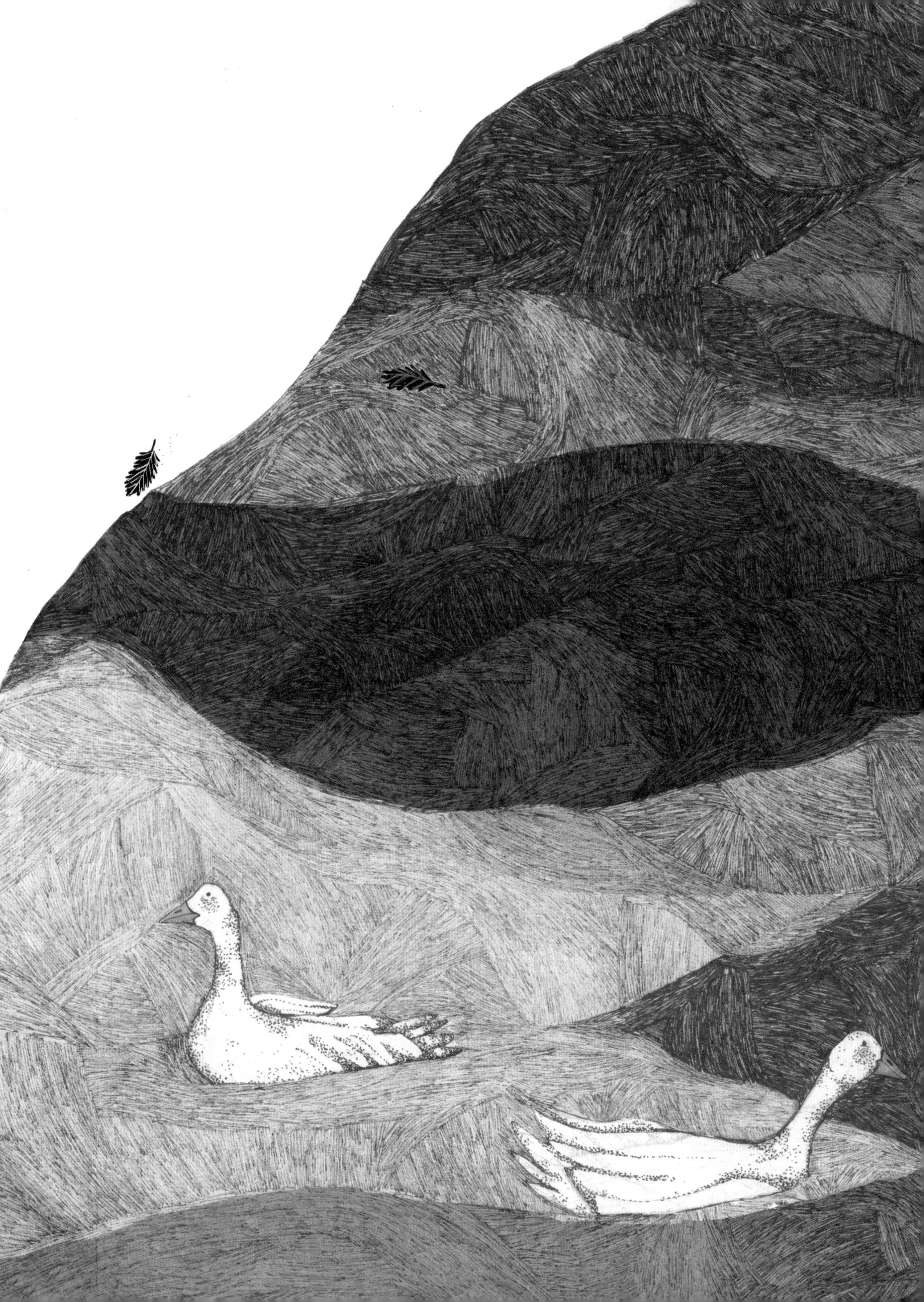

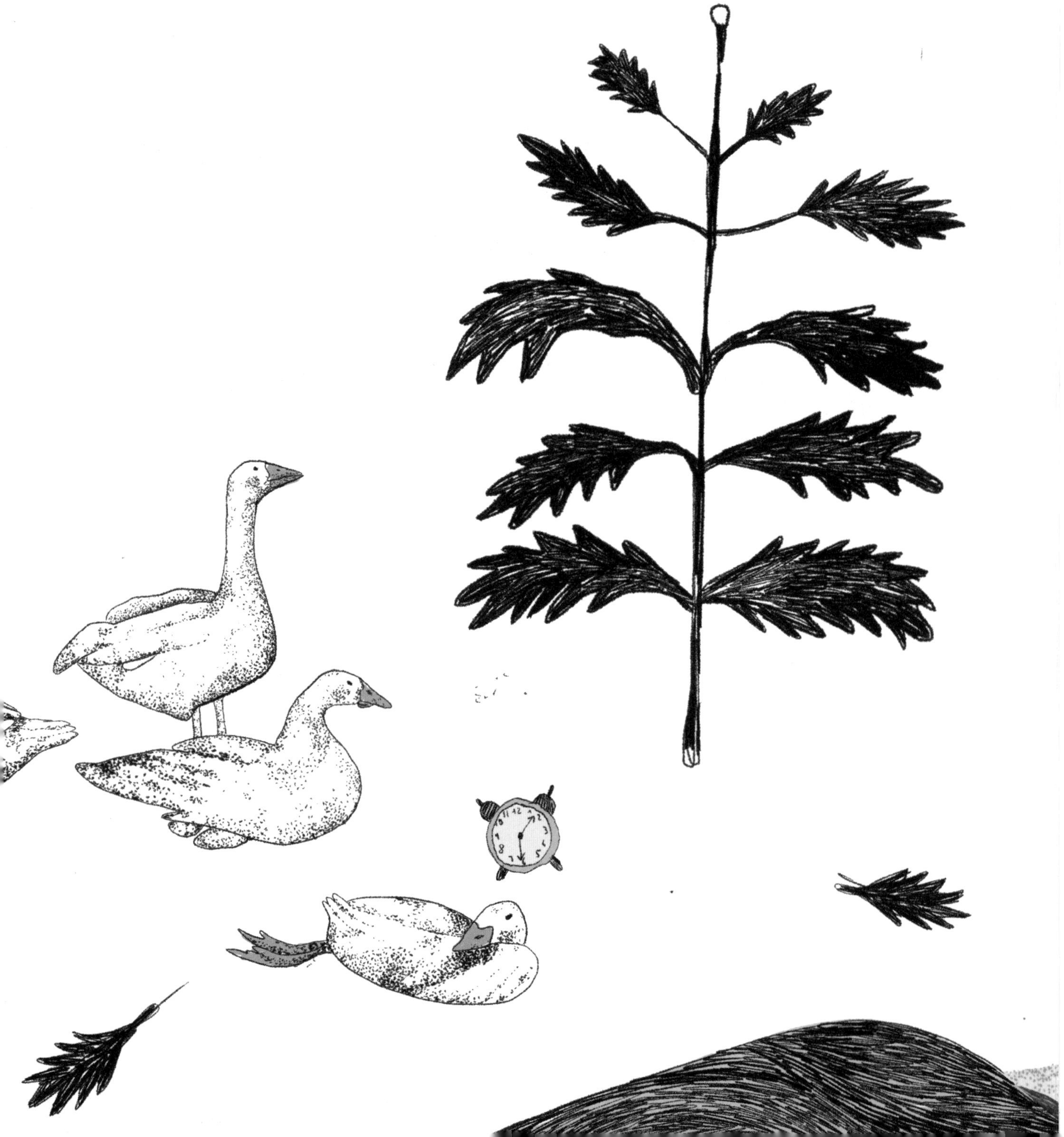
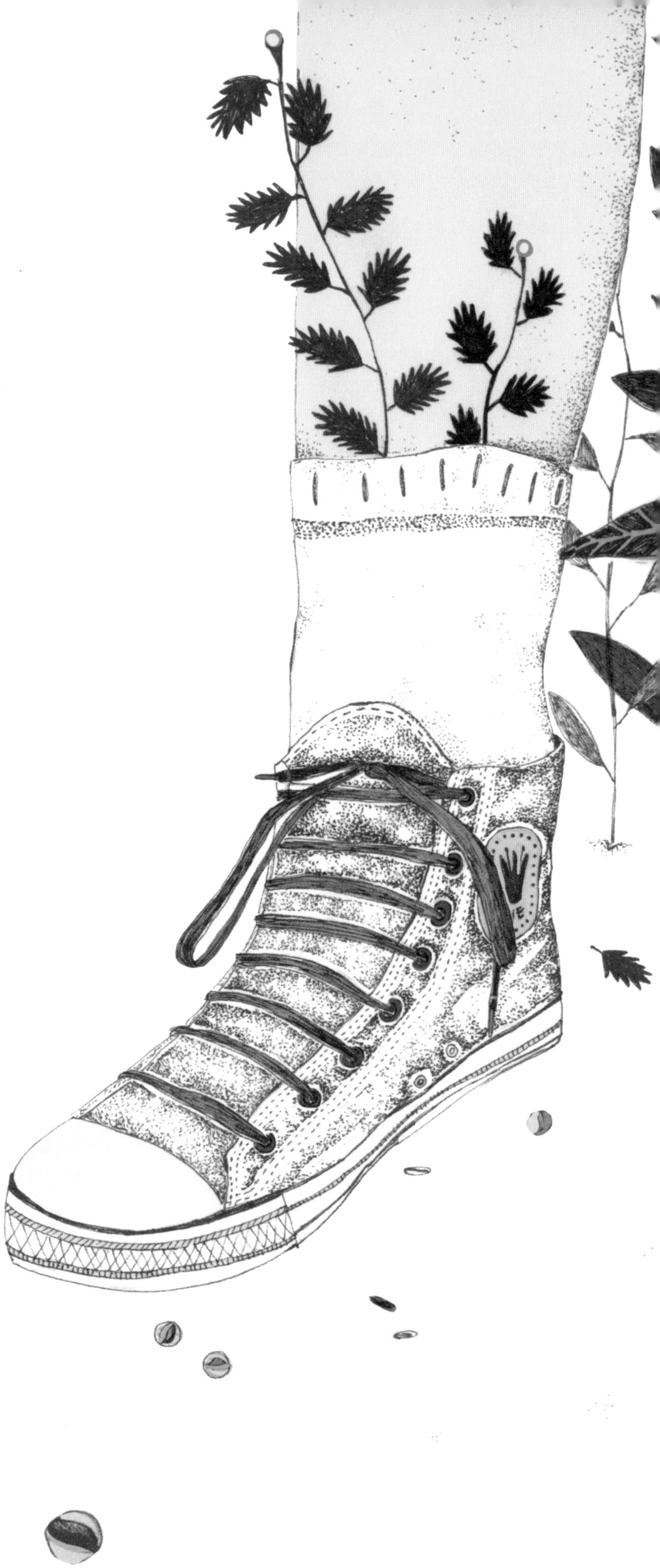

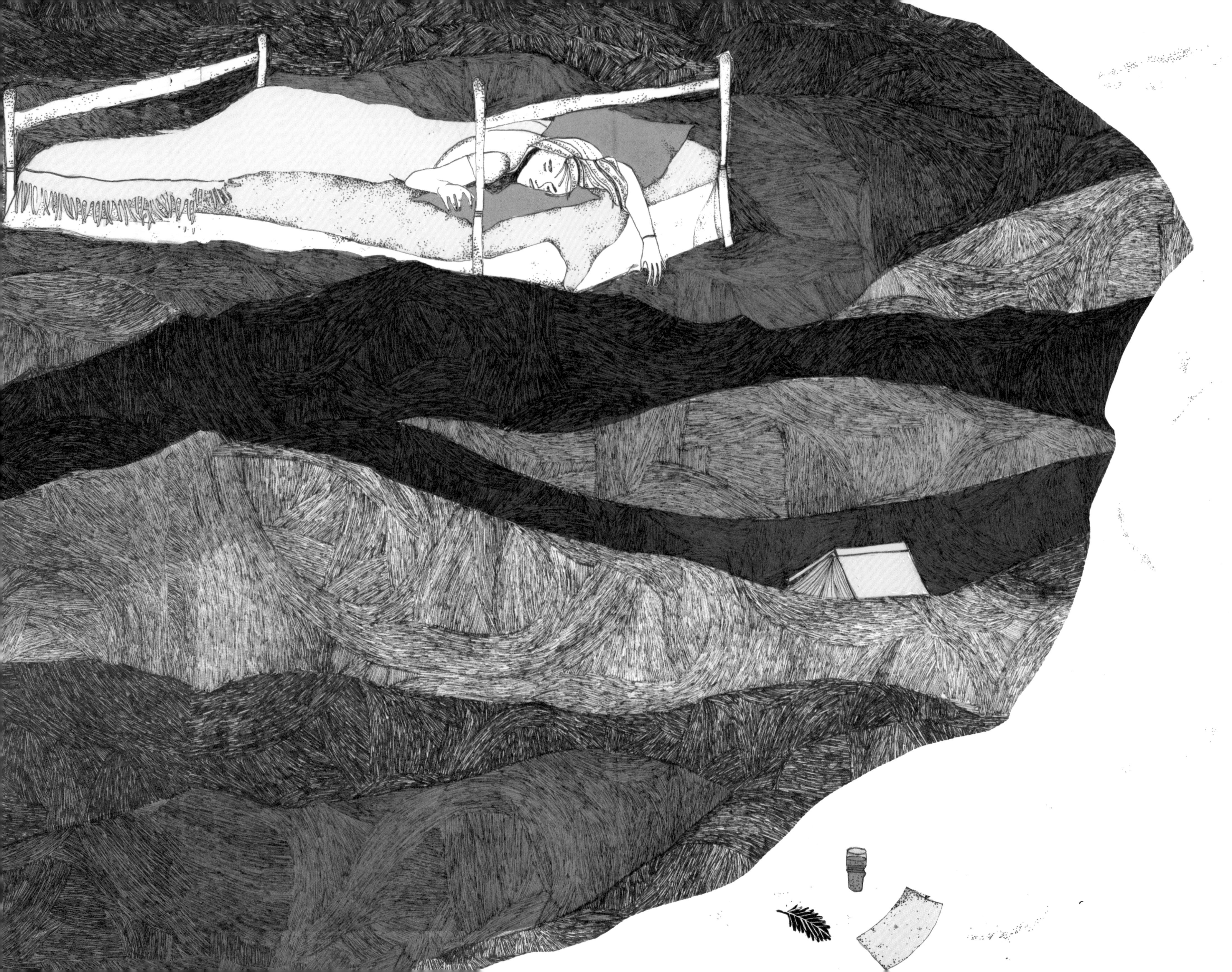

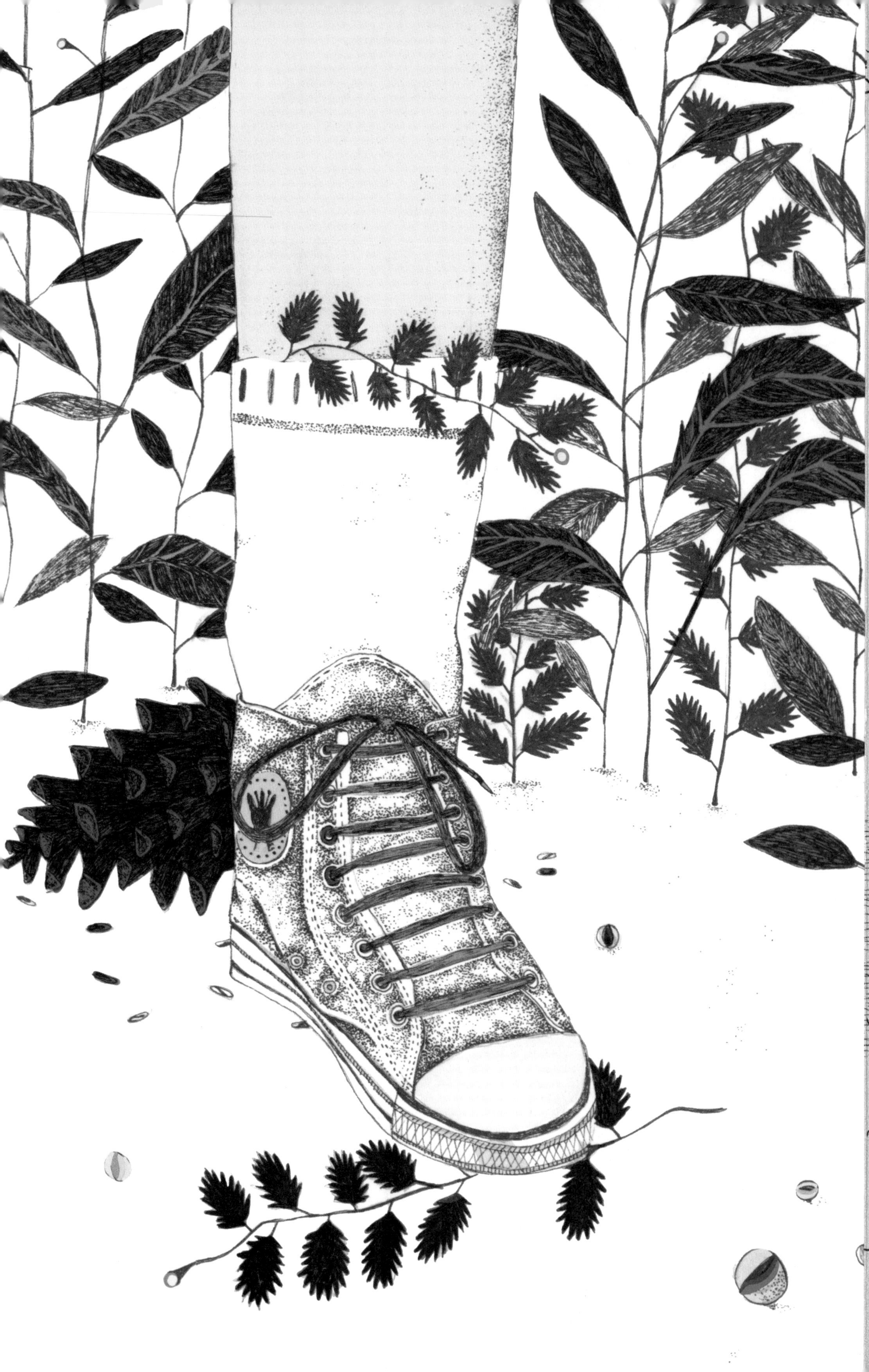

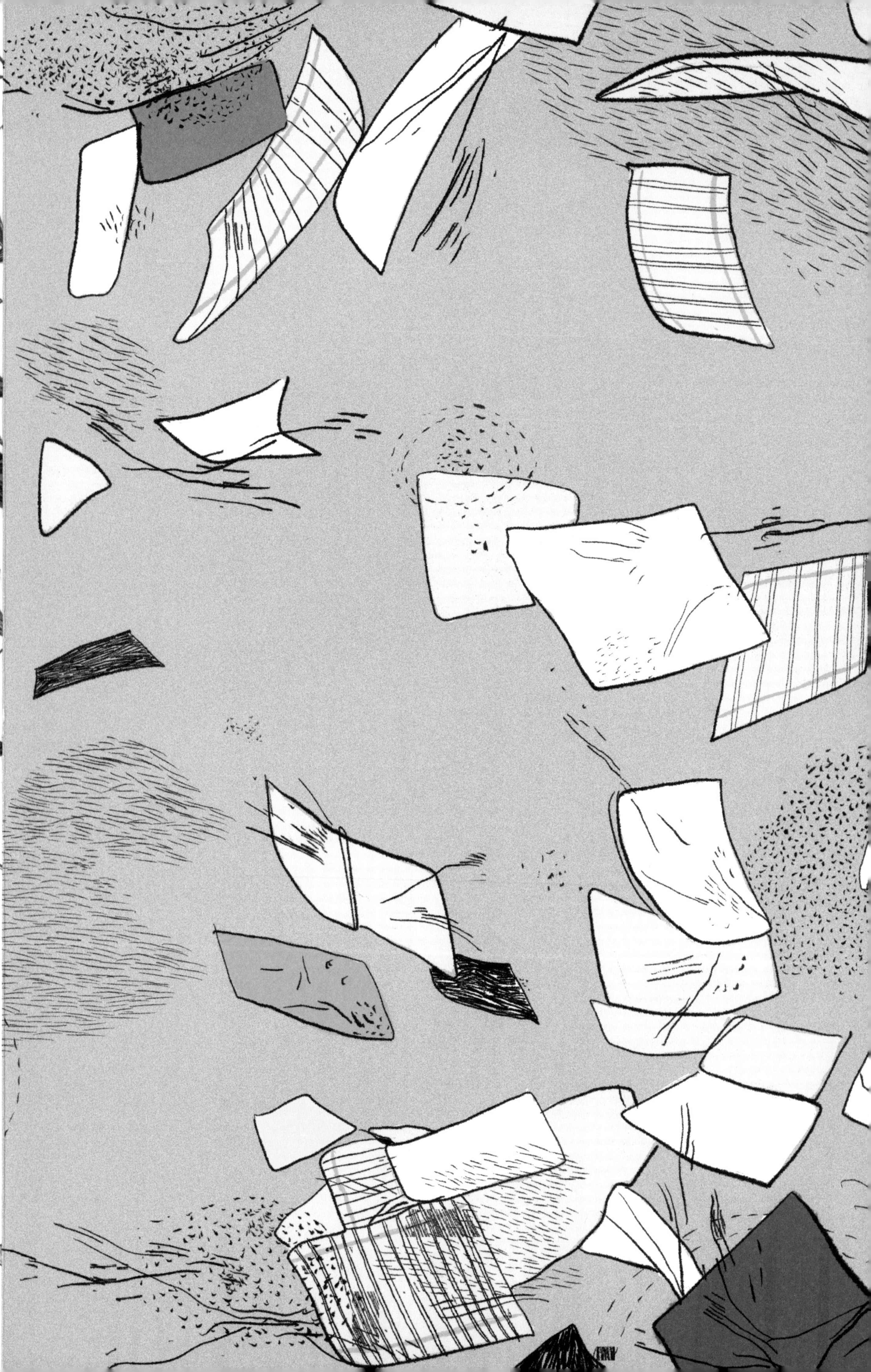

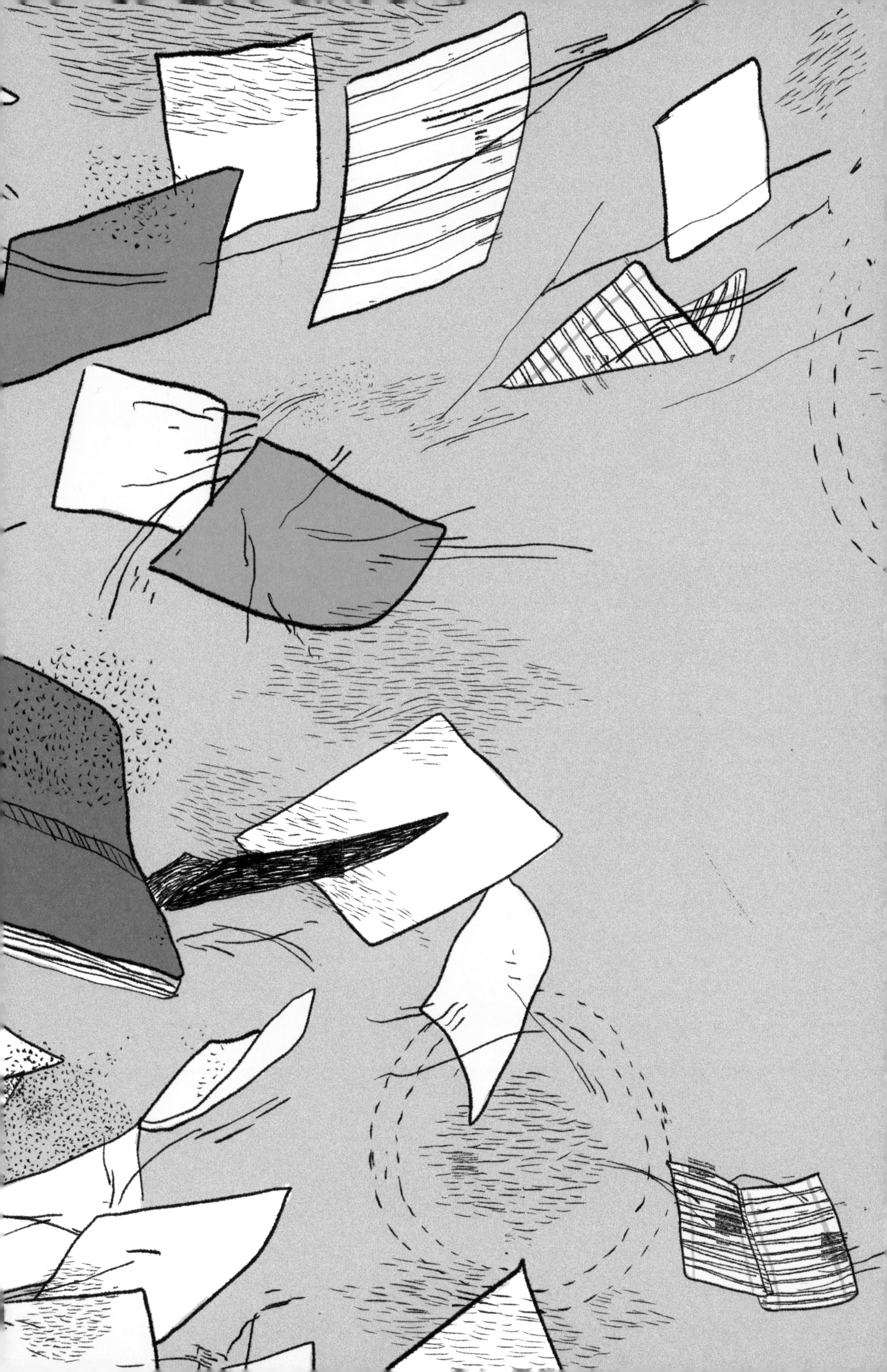

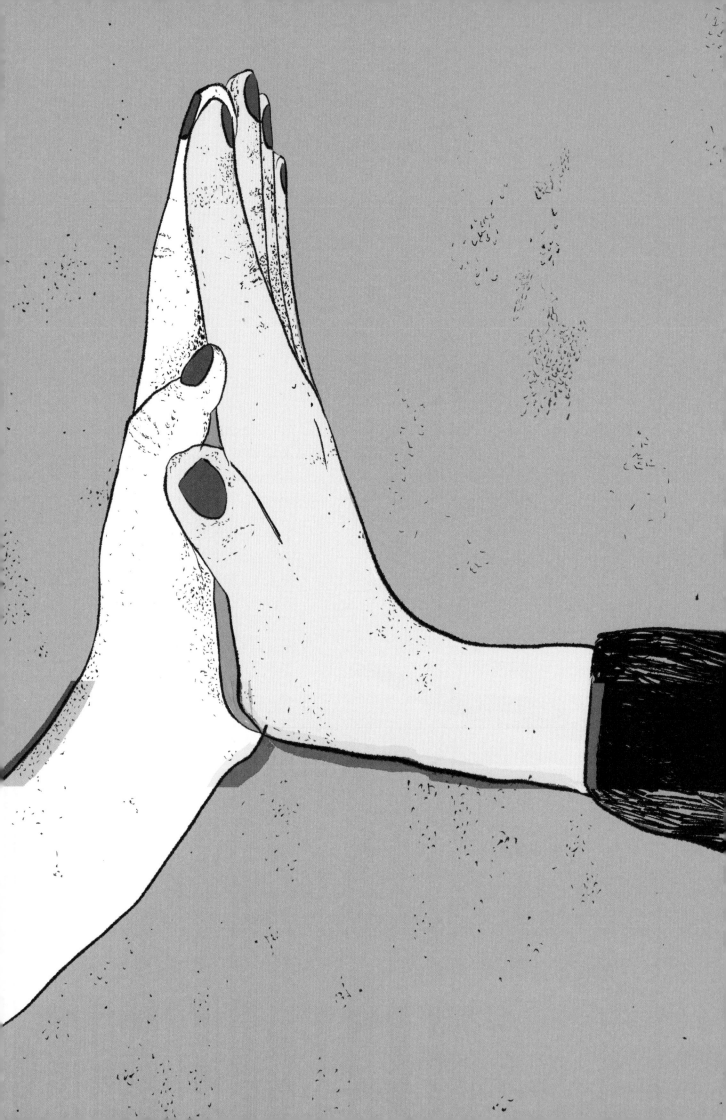

A Seven Stories Press book

Originally published in Polish by Wydawnictwo Format
under the title *Miłość od pierwszego wejrzenia*

Copyright © 2022 by Wydawnictwo Format

All Works by Wisława Szymborska © The Wisława Szymborska Foundation
www.szymborska.org.pl

Copyright illustrations © 2019 by Beatrice Gasca Queirazza

"Love at First Sight" from *Map: Collected and Last Poems* by Wisława Szymborska,
translated from the Polish by Clare Cavanagh and Stanisław Barańczak.

English translation copyright © 2015 by HarperCollins Publishers LLC.

Reprinted by permission of Mariner Books, an imprint of HarperCollins Publishers LLC.k

All rights reserved.

Library of Congress Cataloging-in-Publication Data is on file.

Printed in Poland.

9 8 7 6 5 4 3 2 1

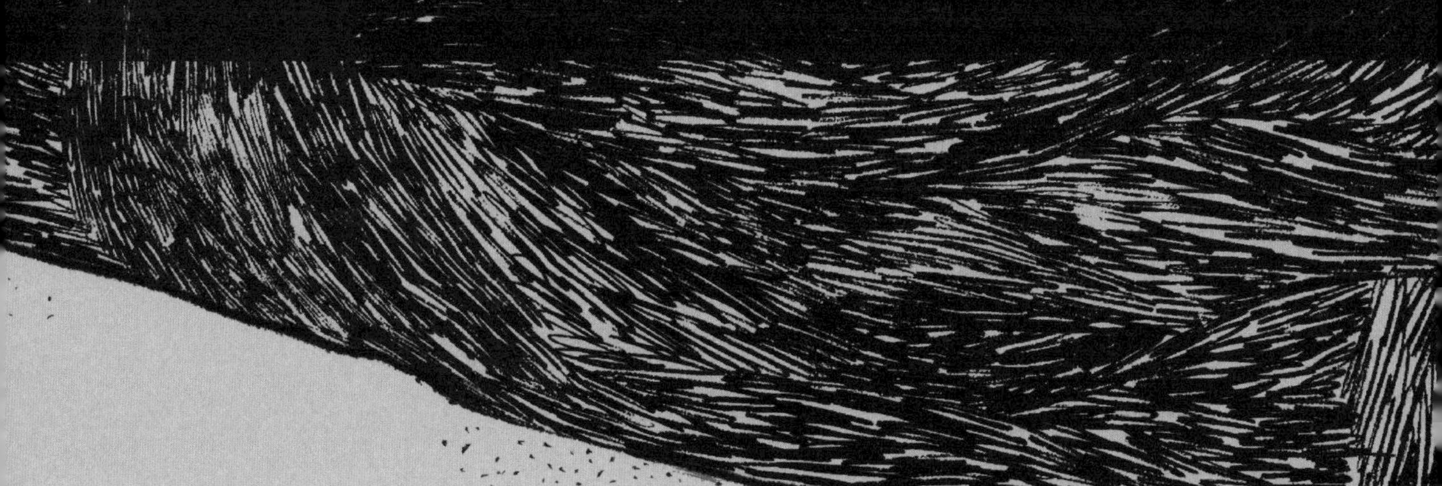

**Wisława Szymborska** (1923-2012) received international recognition when she won the Nobel Prize for Literature in 1996. Collections of her poems that have been translated into English include *People on a Bridge* (1990), *View with a Grain of Sand: Selected Poems* (1995), *Miracle Fair* (2001), *Monologue of a Dog* (2005), and *Map: Collected and Final Poems* (2015) in which the poem "Love at First Sight" first appeared. Szymborska was born in Poland and lived most of her life in Kraków. In addition to the Nobel, she received the Polish PEN Club prize, the Goethe Prize, and the Herder Prize.

**Beatrice Gasca Queirazza** is an Italian illustrator and graphic designer based in Torino, Italy. She studied illustration and animation at Institute European Design in Milan and studied painting and screenprinting at Saint Martin's School in London. Her favorite materials are pencil, ink, collage and digital color.

**Clare Cavanagh** received an NBCC award for criticism and a PEN Translation prize for her work, with Polish poet and translator **Stanisław Barańczak** (1946-2014), on Szymborska's poetry.

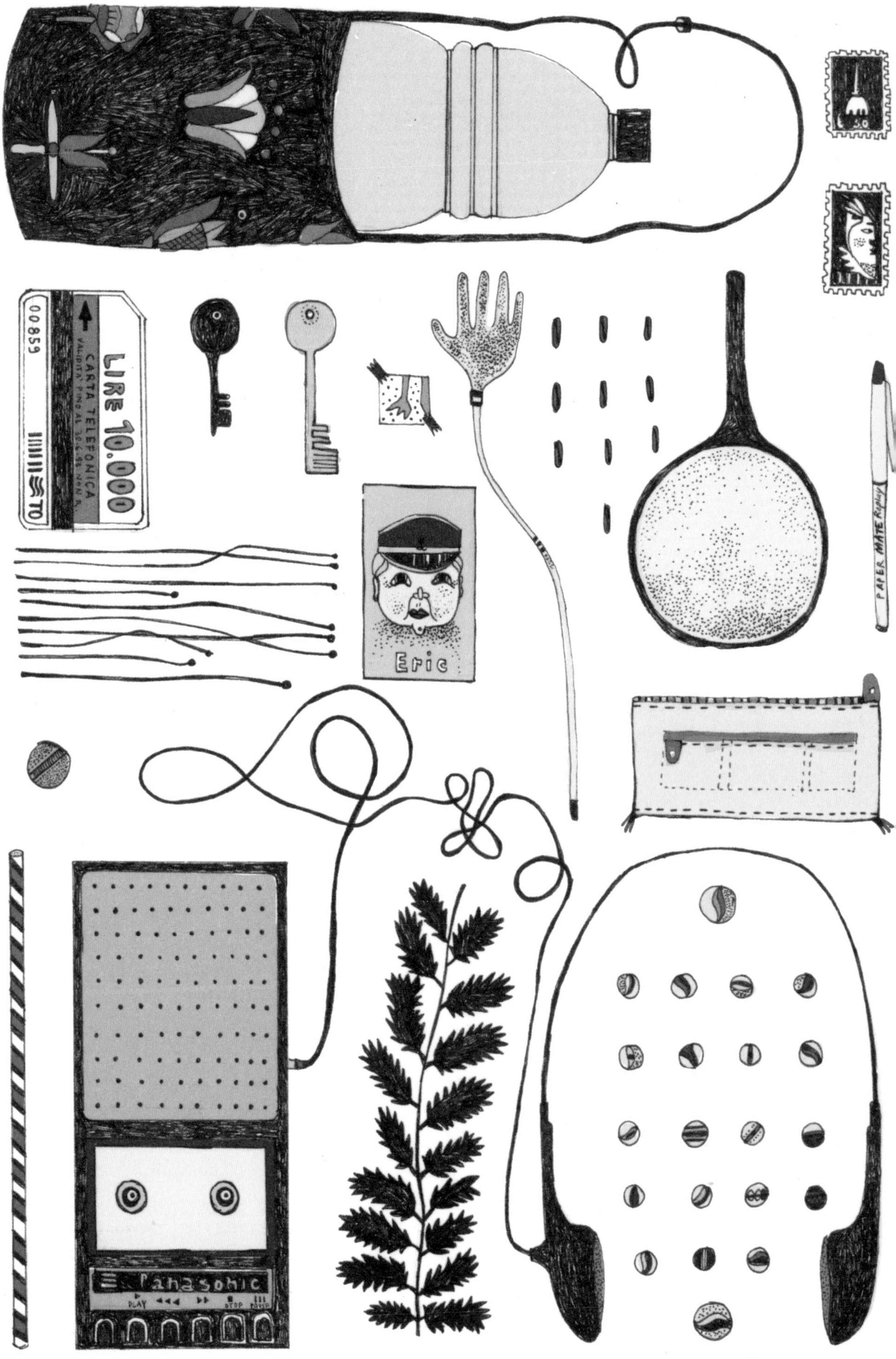
00859
LIRE 10.000
CARTA TELEFONICA
Eric
PAPER MATE Replay
Panasonic
PLAY
STOP